Praise for

A Woman of Pleasure

"With crystalline economy precisely calibrated to a world where money, beauty, power, and the lifeforce of women are measured against the value of pleasure and exchanged for survival, Kiyoko Murata's novel comes alive with exacting force. Reading *A Woman of Pleasure* is like walking into the stratified rooms of Shinonome vibrant with a kaleidoscopic range of perspectives, each drawn with such nuance and sensitivity that they held me as captive as the changing, patriarchal world of early 1900s Japan held this community of women and girls. A marvel."

—ASAKO SERIZAWA, winner of the PEN/Open Book Award and author of *Inheritors*

"Even though *A Woman of Pleasure* exposes the brutal life of sex workers, a dynamic optimism runs throughout the book. Only Kiyoko Murata can convey this world."

—YOKO OGAWA, author of *The Memory Police* (*Yomiuri Shimbun*)

"Ichi Aoi is an honest and open-minded protagonist. She is completely contrary to the stereotypical image of sex workers."

—AKIKO ITOYAMA, author of *In Pursuit of Lavender* (*Yomiuri Shimbun*)

"A book that fully showcases the craft of a veteran writer."
—*Tokyo Shimbun*

"Kiyoko Murata is an excellent storyteller who can make folktales and mythological legends burrow into our psyche, sharply delineating the joy and horror of life and death. The knowledge concerning the inner workings of the female body that is passed on from woman to woman in this book is amazingly powerful."
—*Mainichi Shimbun*

"The conventional novel about Japanese brothels shows only either the glamor or the misery of the place, but this work shows both." —*Hokkaido Shimbun*

"Very impressive work that gives you an idea of the life of a prostitute, often portrayed only as a miserable being."
—*Nihon Keizai Shimbun*

A WOMAN OF PLEASURE

A Woman of Pleasure

A Novel

Kiyoko Murata

TRANSLATED FROM THE JAPANESE BY
JULIET WINTERS CARPENTER

Counterpoint
Berkeley, California

A WOMAN OF PLEASURE

This is a work of fiction. All of the characters, organizations, and events portrayed in this novel are either products of the author's imagination or are used fictitiously.

First published in the Japanese language as YUJOKO by SHINCHOSHA Publishing Co., Ltd., in Tokyo in 2013.

First Counterpoint edition: 2024

Library of Congress Cataloging-in-Publication Data
Names: Murata, Kiyoko, 1945– author. | Carpenter, Juliet Winters, translator.
Title: A woman of pleasure : a novel / Kiyoko Murata ; translated from the Japanese by Juliet Winters Carpenter.
Other titles: Yūjokō. English
Description: First Counterpoint edition. | Berkeley, California : Counterpoint, 2024.
Identifiers: LCCN 2023034737 | ISBN 9781640095793 (trade paperback) | ISBN 9781640095809 (ebook)
Subjects: LCSH: Japan—History—Meiji period, 1868–1912—Fiction. | Courtesans—Japan—Fiction. | LCGFT: Historical fiction. | Novels.
Classification: LCC PL856.U735 Y8513 2024 | DDC 895.63/5—dc23/eng/20230803
LC record available at https://lccn.loc.gov/2023034737

Cover design and illustration by Farjana Yasmin
Book design by Wah-Ming Chang

COUNTERPOINT
2560 Ninth Street, Suite 318
Berkeley, CA 94710
www.counterpointpress.com

Printed in the United States of America

10 9 8 7 6 5 4 3 2 1

Counterpoint gratefully acknowledges support from the Japan Foundation for this publication.

Contents

A WOMAN OF PLEASURE

On the Waves

The girl who came from a southern island in the springtime was fifteen.

She brought with her a couple of patchwork kimonos—any townsperson would have taken them for dustrags—and a few cloths resembling underskirts. That's all her mother had packed for her as she left home, never to return.

The island where the girl was born had steep cliffs on three sides. From the cliff tops, sea turtles could be seen swimming leisurely on the surface of the water below. They were bigger than humans and always stayed together in twos and threes. The seawater was a mix of blue and white, as if milk had spilled into it, because of sulfur from a volcano rising high on the east side of the island, ready to spit fire at any moment.

The girl had left that southern island, sailed around the west side of Satsuma Peninsula, stopping at a couple of ports along the way, and finally, after two days and nights, arrived at Misumi Port in Kumamoto on the big island of Kyushu. It felt to her like a foreign country.

On shore, she discovered streets lined with grand houses the likes of which she had never seen before. She was taken to a particularly large mansion and ushered into a small front room where four girls about her age were sitting, each accompanied by the unsavory man who had brought her there. The men soon left, and one by one the girls were summoned by name. There was a fusuma door and beyond it another room that they were told to enter.

Soon after the first girl went inside and the door slid shut, the others heard her utter a small cry. It wasn't loud but sounded as if she were surprised or choking. A man had been waiting in the room; they heard him whisper, "Hold still." For a little while neither he nor she made a sound, and then in the stillness the other girls heard the faint rustle of clothing.

After a few minutes, the door slid open and the girl reemerged with her hair mussed and the front of her kimono in disarray. She held up the skirt of her kimono in one hand to keep from tripping on it and went to sit in a corner. The next girl was summoned and disappeared behind the door. Again there was the slight exclamation of surprise, or a small scream.

Then it was the turn of the girl from the island.

"Aoi Ichi."

"Yep."

Ichi gulped, got up, and went cautiously into the other room, where a beautiful chubby man in his fifties was sitting cross-legged on a futon, dressed in a kimono of lustrous silk. His jet-black hair was sleek with oil, his complexion fair, his cheeks ruddy; every inch of him glowed with health. To Ichi, who had grown up on an impoverished island, the word "beautiful" applied to people like him. Her father was thin and ugly.

The man gestured for her to come near. She obeyed, attracted to the soft cotton futon like a frog hypnotized by the gaze of a snake. Swiftly he toppled her onto her back and with fluid motions parted her thighs, thrust a warm finger inside her, and then his hot sex. Ichi opened her mouth and softly cried out. It hurt.

The man moved his hips as if counting, *one, two, three* . . . and withdrew when he reached nine or ten. Then he motioned with his chin for her to leave. This was the inspection imposed on all girls purchased by the brothel.

Ichi stood up again. She found it hard to walk, as if something were stuck between her legs. She staggered to the door, opened it, and went out.

The rooms where the girls would live were on the third floor. Newcomers were supplied with personal belongings, bedding, and fresh clothes. "Throw away everything you brought from home," they were told. The new kimonos were beautiful, unlike anything Ichi had ever seen on the island. The other girls all draped theirs over their shoulders and pranced, but Ichi was still shaken by the bizarre ceremony that had taken place in the little room below. These kimonos, prettier even than New Year's kimonos, and these futons stuffed with cotton (back on the island everyone slept on straw)—these fancy things had undoubtedly been given to them in exchange for that ceremony.

Ichi sensed that the thing the man had thrust between her legs in that incredible encounter was the most important thing in this elegant mansion, the thing around which the whole place revolved. It was why an army of servants went briskly about their business, women dressed up, lanterns were lit, and the pavement outside was sprinkled with water. Amid all that activity, rising like a king, was . . . the thing he had inserted into her.

The girls all spoke with heavy accents.

They had been sold here from as far north as the old provinces of Chikuzen and Chikugo, from nearby Hizen and Higo, and from as far south as the Satsuma and Osumi Peninsulas, as well as islands more than thirty miles beyond.

Speaking in your native dialect was forbidden. If they all did that, the brothel staff and customers would be thrown into confusion. Here in the licensed quarter, there was a certain way of speaking that everybody had to use. Ichi's Kagoshima speech sounded to the others like the squawking of a chicken. If you listened carefully, there were traces of the Satsuma-Osumi dialect, but it was a little different. No one could understand her.

Ichi would wave insistently to the other girls and say, "*Koke ko!*" It took two weeks before they realized that that cry like a shrill birdcall meant "Come here." In the refectory, when food was passed out, Ichi would hold out her rice bowl and say, "*Ko, ke!*" This meant "Give me this." What made it all the more confusing was that the same expression could mean "Eat this."

Taciturn by nature, Ichi limited her speech to these odd syllables that sounded to the others like chicken squawks.

The girls weren't put to work right away. They were like vegetables fresh from the field, still muddy: before they could be served, they needed to have the dirt shaken off, have unsightly leaves removed, and be washed clean.

The Kumamoto licensed quarter flourished more than any other in all of Kyushu. Indeed, it was one of the top five in the country, the equivalent of Tokyo's Yoshiwara and Kyoto's Shimabara. The brothel Ichi had been sold to was owned by a man named Hajima Mohei, who controlled the rice market at Dojima in Osaka.

When he appeared in Dojima, a momentary hush fell over the place, people said.

When Mohei returned to Kumamoto, he brought back with him first-class courtesans he had plucked from Yoshiwara and Shimabara, sparing no expense. To maintain high standards, all new girls received strict training. A special few were assigned to an *oiran*, the highest-ranking courtesan, to learn makeup, diction, and manners.

Shinonome from the Shimabara licensed quarter was the most popular courtesan in the place. The brothel was also named the Shinonome; the top earner always took the name of her place of work. Shinonome became Ichi's mentor.

Even though Ichi could barely express herself like a human, one look at her and everyone understood why she had been assigned to Shinonome. On her rocky, volcanic island—the sort of place where stumbling upon a folkloric demon would come as no surprise—inhabitants were descended from two contrasting lines: square-jawed Kagoshima natives and the southernmost remnant of the aristocratic Taira, defeated long ago in the sea battle of Dannoura. Descendants of the latter line were distinguished by their classic oval faces, like Ichi's.

Shinonome smiled as she painted Ichi's lips the red

of the jewel beetle: "Really, you could have been my little sister."

Ichi didn't know that she had been purchased for a higher price than the other newcomers. Besides girls with pretty faces, island girls who could swim were highly valued, especially the daughters of amas, women sea divers.

Shinonome relaxed by the window of her room early one afternoon and watched as Ichi, her face still burned by wind and sun, polished the wooden pillars. When Ichi walked from one pillar to the next, she didn't move like the girls from farming villages. Those girls walked like lizards, with hips turned out, their feet moving forward—right, left, right, left—in parallel lines. Island girls, used to swimming in the sea, walked with their legs close together, their footsteps forming a single straight line. Such girls had sturdy lower bodies.

"What do people catch in the sea around your island?" Shinonome asked.

"Ahkin catch *kē* an' *kēso* an' *io*," Ichi responded, turning to face the oiran. The words verged on incomprehensible. She meant shellfish, seaweed, and fish.

Ichi smiled.

Shinonome smiled back at her.

"Not 'Ahkin' but 'I can.' Repeat after me: 'I can.'"

Ichi repeated the words.

"And what is your name?" Shinonome scratched her head with a long hairpin.

Her eyes on Shinonome, Ichi searched far back in her mind. She had almost forgotten.

"Kojika."

She had just been given this new name. The other new girls also had new names: Kogin, Kikumaru, Hanaji, Umekichi. How they were written she didn't know. She had only been taught the characters for her own name, which meant "little deer."

The girls had much to learn.

Sexual techniques were of paramount importance, so every morning after they had eaten breakfast, tidied the kitchen, and done the cleaning and laundry, they received intensive training in a small upper room spread with futons. The lessons took place under the guidance of Otoku, the old woman who supervised new girls' training. She taught them with a bamboo ruler in hand.

Girls in cheap brothels, not knowing these techniques, yielded the initiative and allowed clients to handle their bodies, those precious commodities, as they pleased. As a result, they lost vitality and suffered injuries to their genitals and elsewhere. To teach her charges how to guide a client as they wished, Otoku took now the role of client, now the role of courtesan, initiating them in techniques that were precise, refined, delicate, and powerful.

They watched with bated breath.

On her way downstairs after one of these dizzying lessons, Ichi caught sight of the blue sky. If she could fly over the rooftops, she might dive deeper and deeper into that sky as into the sea and swim all the way to her island. But Ichi was not a bird, so she could not take wing into the freedom of the sky.

Without permission, the girls could not go through the enormous gate at the end of the street in front of the licensed quarter. Ichi sometimes thought that she might be living in Ryugu-jo, the underwater palace of the god of the sea—a strange Ryugu-jo where no sea bream or flounder danced.

"Goodbye!"

"I'm off!"

After lunch the girls set off for a special school for prostitutes. They each took with them a cloth bundle containing a slate, paper, and a writing box with an ink-stone, ink stick, and brush. Otoku came charging after Ichi and grabbed her by the arm, making her squeal. Ichi looked down at her feet and cringed.

"Where do you think you're going, barefoot?" demanded Otoku.

On the island, no one wore sandals. Ichi studied her feet, the toes exposed to the fresh air. Her teacher, too, would have scolded her if she had gone to school like this.

"Only dogs and cats don't wear sandals!" Otoku shouted.

But on the island, no one did. What's more, her mother and her big sister were amas, and even on land they wore only a narrow loincloth. But Ichi could understand Otoku's anger. Clients did not come here to purchase women who walked around barefoot.

"Are you a dog? A cat? Act like a human!"

Ichi ran back inside to get her sandals and then walked to school with the other girls.

The Female Industrial School was housed in a stylish, modern brick building, with the school's name engraved on a large wooden sign. The brothel owners association had established the school in the spring of 1901, just two years before Ichi arrived, to educate women working in the pleasure quarter. The local newspaper reported that the police chief had spoken at the opening ceremony and as many as 330 prostitutes and barmaids had enrolled.

Regardless of their age, students were sorted by ability into eight classes: plum blossom, cherry blossom, double-flowered cherry blossom, magnolia, peony, wisteria, cotton rose, and bush clover. Six subjects were taught: morality, reading, calligraphy, composition, ikebana, and sewing. Prostitutes attended class a couple of days a week as their schedules allowed.

Ichi and the others were assigned to the peach-blossom class, an additional class that accepted new girls each month. None of them had started working yet, so they attended school almost every day. The peach-blossom class focused on calligraphy and composition. The most urgent needs were correcting the girls' dreadful accents and preparing them to write proper letters to clients with ink and brush. They met in the first room past the entrance, a medium-sized classroom with several rows of long, low writing desks, each seating three, and a thin reed mat that covered the floor.

The girls took out their slates and politely greeted the teacher, a woman in her midforties named Akae Tetsuko. Rumor had it that her father, a direct retainer of the shogun, had fallen on hard times after the collapse of the Tokugawa shogunate and the start of the new Meiji era and had sold her into prostitution in Tokyo's Yoshiwara district. Her back was straight, her way of speaking somehow different. She seldom smiled.

Today's lesson was calligraphy, so Akae Tetsuko wore the sleeves of her kimono neatly bound up to keep them out of the way. She stood in front of the blackboard and wrote two kanji characters in chalk.

"Today we are going to learn to read and write the names for various things in our surroundings," she said. "This is the name of the sun that shines on the earth during the day. In the morning, the sun comes out and makes the world bright. When the sun goes down at night, the world grows dark. The sun is the source of light. Do these characters not give you a sense of strength?" This was her style of teaching.

Next she wrote a single kanji. This, she explained, represented the moon, which came out in the night sky after the sun set and it grew dark out. The moon shone with a beautiful pale light but could not give off light itself.

One by one, she taught them to write basic words: mountain, river, tree, sea, water, wind.

Ichi was attracted to the characters for "sun." They seemed at once solid and showy. By comparison, the one for "moon" looked forlorn, as if the wind could blow right through it and knock it over at any time.

The character for "sea" was messy and complicated. Maybe that was because there was so much life in the sea, she thought, shellfish and fish and seaweed and turtles and dolphins and more. She remembered then that not just sea turtles but pods of dolphins, too, used to swim near the island. They were huge, bigger than her father's boat, but the eyes and mouth in a dolphin's broad face were always smiling. Ichi fondly recalled swimming with dolphins in the sea.

The teacher took up the chalk again and wrote out the kanji for "father," "mother," "older brother," "older sister," "younger brother," and "younger sister." When she explained these words, many of the students had tears in their eyes, remembering their families back home.

"We were each born into this world thanks to our father and mother. You have left home due to unavoidable circumstances, but you must not blame your parents. Whatever pain you feel, the suffering of parents longing for their child is far greater."

The girls were weeping silently. Ichi saw that "sea" contained the character for "mother" and thought of the naked bodies of the amas, paler even than dolphins, swimming together in a sea lit by white rays of the sun.

Yes, her mother was always in the sea. Smaller than a dolphin, larger than a fish, she swam with such lightness and grace that she seemed weightless, but she could dive with the speed of a tornado toward the bottom of the sea. In the water with the other divers, all of them naked except for a loincloth, she was indistinguishable from the rest.

A few of the women had big, bobbling breasts, but mostly their bodies were firmly toned and small-breasted, made for swimming, with nothing extraneous. Out of the water, they had the appearance of young girls. Swimming gave them broad shoulders and powerful arms, but their breasts were those of a girl of fifteen or sixteen, and because they held their breath during dives, their abdomens were as flat and taut as a young man's.

A tear fell onto the character for "sea" in front of Ichi.

"Now take out your slate and write your name," the teacher said. "I taught you how the other day, so I am sure you can do it."

Ichi wrote "Aoi Ichi" in clumsy letters. Her name looked like a row of little fish. Not characters but small living things holding their breath. *This is me*, she thought, staring. *All of me. My coming from the island, my being sold here.* Her entire story was there in "Aoi Ichi." She wanted to caress the letters.

The girl to her right wrote "Matsuyama Setsu," the girl to her left "Tanaka Riu." They had all been told that when asked their name, they must answer from now on with the new name assigned to them by the brothel owner, that they must forget their real name. But at school, the teacher taught them to write their real names first of all. This was essential, so that they could each read the promissory note stating the terms of their debt.

The owner of the establishment where Akae Tetsuko, their teacher, was once sold hadn't known what to do with her, people said. As the educated daughter of a Tokugawa samurai, she'd had a habit of talking back to him and the clients both. Her complexion was dark, her forehead unusually large and prominent, her eyes small and deep-set with a piercing gaze. She had attracted no clients. Her only talents were calligraphy and reading the *Analects* of Confucius. In the end she'd worked in the kitchen, in the laundry, and on accounts, with a period of servitude twice as long as normal.

When she was finally released, she drifted to Hakata in Kyushu and worked as a bookkeeper in the pleasure quarter of Yanagimachi, where Hajima Mohei of the Shinonome reached out to her. Perhaps no one was more qualified than Akae Tetsuko to teach in the Female Industrial School.

"Now write the name you were given here," she said. The girls erased their real names from their slates and wrote out their new names with a clatter of chalk.

Ichi could not remember the kanji for her new name and wrote it phonetically in kana instead. The girls on either side of her wrote their names in kanji that were ungainly but correct.

"What is this? I taught you just yesterday." The teacher wrote "Kojika" on Ichi's slate.

"I ain't a deer."

"It's okay," said the girl called Kogin. "Just means you're cute like a little deer, right?"

Ichi did not look pleased.

The teacher told them to put away their slates. "Now take out a sheet of paper and grind some ink." She ended each lesson by having them write a journal entry. "Do not try to write fine phrases. Write whatever you please, just as if you were talking to me."

Long ago when the teacher had been sold, a friend sold with her brought along *Collection of Poetry Old and New* and other works of classical literature inherited from her mother, tucked inside a bundle of clothes. Those books, which the two of them read from every day, had served as a lamp lighting their way across a sea of troubles. The year her friend fulfilled her Yoshiwara contract, a young man with a degree from Tokyo Imperial University, the son of a former retainer of the Tosa domain, had fallen in love with her and married her. She had gone with him to Germany. What might her life be like now?

"Whatever happens, let's hold our heads high," they had promised each other as they exchanged books.

Returning from far-off days, the teacher looked from the window to the desks where the girls sat. Aoi Ichi had finished writing and held out her paper. *This one always shoves her paper at me like a challenge. She is a bossy little thing.*

May 15 Aoi Ichi
Forgot my sandals,
got called a dog, a cat.
My pa and ma they
go barefoot on the island.

Here I wear sandals.

Does wearing sandals make you human?

Akae Tetsuko looked at Ichi and visualized the girl's parents, living their lives half-naked on the island. She was silent, not knowing what to say. She could already tell that this was a girl with a strong independent mind.

School ended at three thirty. From then until around six in the evening, the girls bathed and dressed themselves with care.

One day, Ichi caused an incident.

After school, she returned as usual to the room of the oiran Shinonome, announcing herself at the door. Instead of her former incomprehensible bird talk, she could now say things in passable Japanese.

When she slid open the fusuma, there was Shinonome lying on the futon with her legs spread wide, as Murasaki, the other oiran, removed her pubic hair. At the sight of Shinonome's long white legs, Ichi gasped and started to retreat into the hallway. Still lying on her back, Shinonome beckoned her in with a smile.

"It's fine. Sit down and watch."

"Yes'm." Ichi sat down.

"A woman doesn't need to take care of only her face," said Shinonome. "A hairy groin is unsightly and interferes in bed. Shaving with a razor leaves stubble that could scratch the client, so tweezers are best."

Every time Murasaki pulled out a hair, Shinonome stifled a cry and grimaced. Murasaki handled the tweezers expertly, pulling out hair after hair without pause.

As Ichi looked on, she was reminded of adults on the shore of the island mending fishing nets. If the nets were torn, the precious catch would get away, so when the nets were brought ashore, everyone would spread them out to dry and become absorbed in sewing them with needle and thread. Were fishnets and Shinonome's crotch the same?

Murasaki left a tuft of hair at the top and nodded in satisfaction. "Quite chic!"

Shinonome's hairless crotch looked like a white squid topped with eyelashes. A bit disgusting, really.

After that, Shinonome got up and, smoothing her hair with one hand, looked at Ichi as if struck by a sudden idea. Ichi squirmed.

"I know! Show me yours. I haven't seen it once since you came here, but you've got jet-black hair on your head, so down below must be a fright." With gentle pressure, Shinonome urged her to lie down.

Ichi leaped backward. "No'm, not me."

"You'd rather old Otoku did it? She can be quite brutal."

Murasaki took up the tweezers again and pulled Ichi by the hand.

Hair removal is hard to do on one's own. To avoid the risk of accidental injury, the brothel girls turned to one another for assistance.

"Don't touch me!" said Ichi in her dialect.

With surprising strength in her slender arms, Murasaki grabbed Ichi and twisted her down. Together she and Shinonome turned her on her back and pried open her legs, holding them down on either side. Ichi screeched helplessly, as if she were being throttled.

"What're ya doin'!" she howled. With all her might she kicked Murasaki in the face and sent her flying. Using her other leg she landed a kick on Shinonome's chest, knocking her over, then sprang to her feet and fled the room with the front of her kimono wide open.

"Kojika is running away!" Murasaki shrieked as Ichi thudded down the stairs.

The mighty kick from a trained swimmer left Murasaki's cheek red and swollen, while Shinonome, having taken a direct blow to her chest, lay prostrate, unable to move. At the bottom of the stairs, attracted by the commotion, the broad-shouldered manager stood barring the way. He captured Ichi and held her, but not for long.

Ichi sank her teeth into one of the arms holding her in a pinion, and with a cry the manager relaxed his grip.

She flew outside barefoot and was overpowered by several other men. They tied her to a pillar in the kitchen.

Shinonome was having trouble catching her breath, which caused a fresh uproar. A doctor was sent for. Luckily, she was all right, but she and Murasaki both were forced to go on leave. If either of them had suffered a broken rib, the loss would have been enormous.

The manager went to report the girl's unpardonable savagery to the owner.

Hajima Mohei came out and smacked Ichi four or five times with his fist.

When she saw stars and became dizzy, he shouted in her ear, "Listen to me—straighten yourself out and do as you're told, or you won't die in your bed!"

This was no idle threat. Fed up with the violence of the fifteen-year-old, Mohei was speaking half in earnest.

Ichi had gone limp, so the rope was untied. They wanted to avoid damage to this young girl's body, a valuable commodity.

The teacher looked at the doorway in wide-eyed surprise.

Kogin, Kikumaru, Hanaji, and Umekichi all looked up from their work. It was early afternoon, and they were in the middle of a writing lesson.

Ichi slipped in like a small shadow. Everyone knew

about her rampage, and they stared at her, stunned. Her face still bore purple bruises and her lip was cut.

"You're here to study, aren't you?" The teacher put an arm around her shoulders.

Ichi nodded and took her place. She looked around at the others and followed their example by taking out some paper and grinding ink on her inkstone.

Everyone treated Ichi gingerly. Next to her, Kogin started to say something but decided against it.

Ichi craned her neck and read what Kogin had written.

May 18 Tanaka Riu
This morning a package came from home
Patched underkimono patched underskirt straw sandals
Whatll I do with em?

Poor families couldn't send their daughters anything of value. Ichi found this amusing and burst out laughing. She straightened the paper in front of her and picked up her brush. Then she turned her swollen eyes to the window and saw that again today the sun was shining bright in the blue sky.

She moved her brush across the page with determination.

May 18 Aoi Ichi
The owner talked to me.
Hes wrong.
I wont die in my bed
Ill die on the waves.

The teacher, Kogin, Kikumaru, Hanaji, and Umekichi all looked over Ichi's shoulder and marveled at what she had written.

When Ash Falls, I Remember

One month passed, then another. The girls who had arrived at the same time as Ichi were put on display like vegetables made presentable by washing off their mud and smoothing their leaves. Arrayed in silk kimonos with their hair done up, their faces shaved and powdered, and their lips rouged, no one would have taken them for poor country girls recently sold into prostitution.

Only Ichi, the island girl, had yet to start work. In the daytime Kogin, Kikumaru, Hanaji, and Umekichi wrote on their slates alongside her at school, but in the evening they sat behind the wooden lattice out front, beginning to take customers, while in her little room upstairs Ichi enjoyed the sound sleep of childhood, arms and legs flung wide, oblivious to the breathtaking sexual exploits of the oiran and her patron a short distance away.

Ichi was too young by a couple of years to take customers, but that wasn't the only reason. The brothel owner, Hajima Mohei, had plans for her. Prostitutes came in a variety of ranks. There were implicit ranks for women in ordinary society, too, but among women of pleasure the rankings were explicit and cruel, since they involved assignment of monetary value. The men who frequented the establishment naturally came in various ranks as well. For one of them to choose her, a prostitute needed to meet certain standards.

Only men with money in their pockets could pass through the great red gate at the entrance to the pleasure quarter. Beyond the gate was a wasteland on the outskirts of town. No brothels stood there; a river that was dark at night flowed by, and every so often its waters would yield the body of a prostitute who had thrown herself in. Women stood under the willows on the bank, each with a straw mat under her arm, and accosted passing men: "Come spend some time with me, why don't you?"

These prostitutes of the lowest grade who showed up at nightfall were called "nighthawks" or "hill buns." A man whose pockets were nearly empty could buy one of them for ten sen and do his business with her at the side of the road.

Inside the great gate, shelter and a woman could be had for the night for as little as one yen, thirty sen. At a slightly better place, one that offered food and drinks, the charge was two or three yen. At a first-class brothel, the favors of the reigning oiran—the one who bore the name of the establishment—had no fixed price. At that exalted level, the costs involved were at once hazy and solemnly real. Specially favored patrons, those who paid a fee granting them exclusivity, were not charged by the night. Instead, they paid the ordinary living expenses of the oiran, her followers, and her staff, as well as the costs of her luxurious lifestyle. The food Ichi ate, the clothes she wore, and the leisure she enjoyed were all paid for by Shinonome's patrons.

Hajima Mohei's dream was to nurture a cadre of superior courtesans, young women who could, in bed, send a customer to heaven with secret techniques and, out of bed, charm him with their knowledge of books and poetry and their skill in an array of arts, including dance and tea ceremony.

What set an oiran apart first of all was the body she'd been born with. Beauty and good health were of course important, but more crucial was the configuration of her private parts. Mohei used the classifications "excellent," "good," and "mediocre"; below "mediocre" was "inferior," which needless to say was disqualifying. Above "excellent" were the two highest grades, "superior" and "exceptional." Ichi had been ranked "exceptional."

"Who, that wild monkey of a girl?" Tose, the mistress of the brothel, shook her head in disbelief. Only her husband, Mohei, who had personally assessed Ichi's body on that first day, could make the determination.

"No more running around barefoot like a monkey

or a dog or a cat now," Tose told Ichi, watching her polish the floor outside Shinonome's room. "Do everything the oiran tells you and learn all you can from her." The girl's posture shocked her. *Why, she's like a dog with its head down and bottom up.* "Crouch down when you polish the floor!" She gave Ichi's upended rear a slap.

"Learn?" Ichi said uncertainly. "Learn what?"

"Everything!" called Shinonome in a lilting voice. "How to clean and walk and speak; how to sew and how to read; how to perform the tea ceremony and write poetry. All that and more."

"Why should I learn all that stuff?"

"Because you need to know more than ordinary women do."

Ichi couldn't understand. What could a prostitute who learned such things hope to become? A woman skilled in calligraphy and poetry would know more than the wives of oiran patrons. Ichi found the idea of such a paragon terrifying and repellent. What good could it possibly do for *her* to become like that?

Ichi's mother was skilled at catching fish and shellfish in the sea, but on shore, she barely knew how to talk. She had no need to talk properly to people. She knew nothing about reading or writing. Such knowledge would have served no purpose.

Ichi paused in her cleaning and looked up at Shinonome, thinking again how much the oiran's milk-white skin reminded her of a squid. "I'll tell you this, my ma never asks for money from nobody." Her mother was not in bondage. "And she feeds my pa and us."

Her mother spent no money on herself and kept her family fed. Amas usually earned more than their husbands. Compared to the lives of prostitutes, who sold their bodies by the hour, Ichi didn't think her mother's life was at all pitiable.

Gracious and rarely angry, Shinonome smiled coyly. "I see! Then your mother does it for free? Poor thing . . . She has to work all day every day, getting burned black in the sun, and on top of that she has to sleep with your father at night—and get paid nothing?"

Her face delicate, pale, and luminous, her eyes wide in amazement, Shinonome was more and more like a white giant squid.

"Listen to me, Kojika. Remember this. A prostitute entertains a client only for an agreed-upon time. That's called a contract. When the time is up, the client leaves. Then all there is for her to do is put away the futon in relief. The rest of her time belongs to her and so does her body. The way I see it, there's nobody in the world as free as a prostitute."

Ichi fell silent. She started to think Shinonome might be right. Her head was spinning.

Shinonome went on. "Wives, on the other hand, have to wait on their husbands constantly. The husband pushes his wife down whenever he feels like it and doesn't pay her a penny. She's forced to bear children and work like a pack animal. Pack animals get no pay. All they get is a little food. How is your mother back home any different from a horse or a cow?"

Ichi couldn't speak. *No!* she protested silently. The picture Shinonome's words painted was all wrong. Her mother, with her dusky complexion, breasts like small hard fruits, and firm lean hips, was like the spirit of a fish—nothing like a horse or a cow. Horses and cows were led around by the nose, but her mother wasn't led around by her father. She was the one doing the leading.

Shinonome was clever with words. Smart. Who was cleverer, Ichi wondered—Shinonome or the schoolteacher, Akae Tetsuko?

Ichi had mastered a great many characters. She could write the characters for *shika*, "deer," in "Kojika" (eleven strokes); *gin*, "silver," in Kogin's name (fourteen strokes); and *kiku*, "chrysanthemum," in Kikumaru's name (eleven strokes). But the twenty-stroke character for *tetsu*, "iron," in their teacher's name was beyond her.

"You do not need to be able to write my name," said Tetsuko, her kimono sleeves tied up neatly as usual. "We will learn words that are necessary in your lives."

The characters needed to write letters to favored clients were the only ones useful to a prostitute. If they looked like bent nails or wiggly worms, the client would be repulsed. However, if a steady client took it upon himself to redeem her debts and marry her, she might well end up a wealthy merchant's second wife. Such things happened. Education could equip a prostitute to embark on a new life.

A porter came by daily to gather letters written by women of the licensed quarter and deliver them. Shinonome, Murasaki, and other high-tier courtesans each wrote four or five letters in beautiful calligraphy every day—love letters. Every morning, Shinonome would read aloud what she had written, saying this helped her determine where the phrasing was awkward or repetitious.

> Ever since parting from you on the night of the harvest moon, my heart has been inexplicably heavy, my mind far from serene. I beg of you, from now on spare me visits on evenings lit by brilliant moonbeams. Lovers' parting should rather take place on a pitch-dark night, I think. In the pitch dark, nothing is visible; after parting there is only gloom as, alone in my room, I am filled with darkness, a darkness of the heart that I wish may continue until the end of my days.
>
> I cannot wait to see you again. Each day is like a thousand years.
>
> Shinonome

What a pack of lies! Ichi said to herself, mentally sticking out her tongue. She didn't understand all the words, but something about them set her teeth on edge, made her feel awkward. Shinonome hated all things dark and dismal. She was a rare kind of woman, unfailingly cheerful, with a voice like a canary even when she was crying. The perfection of the bright, round full moon suited her. If her client came on a night when the moon was full, then at the next full moon he would be sure to remember her face and be unable to stay away, Ichi thought.

"How was that?" Shinonome asked, leaning on the writing desk and holding the end of the brush in her mouth.

"All right," Ichi said cheekily.

Shinonome sighed. "A love letter is the hardest thing to write. You definitely have to picture someone you care for as you write it. That's the secret."

"Really?" Ichi's eyes widened. Then, remembering, she said, "I wrote one, too." She ran to her room and in high spirits brought back a piece of paper.

"Well, well," said Shinonome. "Go on, read it to me."

"Yes'm." Ichi seated herself and read aloud in a clear voice.

When ash falls I remember you
the master of the sea.

If you were human
youd be a handsome guy.

The letter was written in her native dialect. To Shinonome it was gibberish. "I haven't the slightest idea what any of that means," she said, shaking her head. "Who on earth were you writing to?"

"A huge sea turtle back home."

Shinonome closed her mouth. *I took her on as my protégée, but when oh when will she ever learn to talk like a human being? The owner says the mouth under her skirt is top quality, but the one at this end is hopeless!*

Anyone whose writing was as garbled as Kojika's would have to have the old porter ghostwrite letters for her. Like Akae Tetsuko, the porter was a member of the samurai class, and her writing style was stiff and formal, hardly suited to love letters. Instead of "I miss you so much and I pine for your return," for example, she would write, "Time passes in vain in my empty room. I look forward to your early return." The porter's services were called on only for prostitutes who were still illiterate.

During writing class one afternoon, Tetsuko looked over the students' journals. She knew at a glance the author of the messy lines written in small, wriggly letters. It had to be Aoi Ichi, the girl from the southern island.

July 1 Aoi Ichi

My ma gathers shellfish and fish in the sea.
She bore my big brother my big sister me
my little brother my little sister.
She works hard and feeds us all.
If shes the same as a cow and a horse
I think cows and horses are great.

Tetsuko smiled discreetly. Aside from Kumamoto, Tetsuko knew only Tokyo, back when it used to be called Edo, and Hakata. What an ama on an island farther south than Kyushu might look like was beyond her imagination. Her mind conjured the hazy figure of a half-naked woman with black hair dripping wet, but the woman had no face.

She called to Ichi, who was busy writing something. "Aoi Ichi. A human mother is not the same as a cow or a horse."

"No, but my oiran said so."

"Your oiran has probably never seen a cow or a horse." Frowning, Tetsuko turned to the next page of Ichi's journal.

July 2

A horse pulled a heavy load down the road.
My oiran saw that and said

"Oh how hard the horse works! We are all the
same."
Its true.
Theres all kinds of work in the world
and some that horses surely dont know.

This time Tetsuko laughed a little. She felt some sympathy for Shinonome, under constant observation by a girl as sharp-eyed as Ichi.

"Aoi Ichi, try finding more beautiful things to write about." Love letters from a courtesan needed to have a certain charm. Look at the flowers blooming now in the garden, she advised the class: hydrangea, Chinese bellflower, lily, amethyst, four-o'clock, gardenia, phlox. Learning to write their difficult but beautiful names would greatly increase the emotional depth of the girls' letters.

Ichi raised her hand. "Ma'am?"

"Yes, what is it?"

"Takenoha isn't listening. She's doing sums."

The student seated at the desk next to Ichi's had joined the class two weeks before. She wasn't young, probably in her late twenties. Her features were even, but she was quite thin. Until recently, she had been working in the pleasure quarter in Osaka. Changing quarters inevitably meant being saddled with fresh debt.

Takenoha resignedly handed over her notebook.

Below each date was a detailed record of her clients for that day. Tetsuko was drawn in.

June 30, 1903
10 p.m.–9 a.m. Kinosuke, dry-goods clerk, Kisaragi-cho, 1 yen 20 sen.

July 1
Saw off Kinosuke. 11:30 a.m.–3 p.m. Karoku, fishmonger, Nishiki-machi, 35 sen. 7 p.m.–9 p.m. Toji, carpenter, Bessho-cho, 40 sen. 10:30 p.m.–10 a.m. Masagoro, livestock dealer, Kawase village, 1 yen 50 sen.

July 2
Saw off Masagoro. 3 p.m.–9 p.m., farmer, Funagoshi village, 1 yen 10 sen. 9:30 p.m.–8 a.m. Gohei, Aone-cho, 1 yen 60 sen.

July 3
Saw off Gohei. 8 a.m.–10:30 a.m., fresh-fish dealer, 60 sen. 5 p.m.–1 a.m. two clients: Masagoro, livestock dealer, Kawase village, 1 yen 60 sen, and Takichi, carpenter, Sakae-cho, 1 yen 60 sen.

"And what is this?"

"A record of the business I've done." Takenoha

spoke without a trace of embarrassment. "I have to keep a careful record because I don't trust the brothel's bookkeeping. I want to pay off my debt as soon as I can and leave this place."

Indeed, some brothels took advantage of prostitutes' illiteracy by fudging the records of their earnings and their remaining debt as specified on the promissory notes recalculated every year. Their bodies abused through constant overwork, year after year such women were burdened with an inconceivable amount of increased debt. For them, the door to freedom remained closed.

The Kagetsu, where Takenoha worked, was a second-rate brothel without any high-ranking courtesans. Such places did not teach their girls to protect their bodies in bed. Tetsuko was aghast at Takenoha's daily workload. Sleeping with, on average, two daytime clients and one all night long allowed scarcely any time to rest. And on the night of July 3, she had entertained two clients, going back and forth between them.

"Working this hard will destroy your health," Tetsuko warned, lowering her voice. Teachers were not allowed to interfere in the prostitutes' work.

"But I'm in a hurry. I work with my eyes closed."

The owner of the Kagetsu did not take kindly to girls in his employ learning to read. However, he was unable to keep them away from the Female Industrial School, since the monthly examinations for sexually transmitted diseases, that great enemy of sex workers, also fell under the school's jurisdiction.

"Ma'am, would you please write out the readings for these characters in kana?" Takenoha took a wrinkled piece of paper from the front of her kimono and spread it out carefully on the desk. It bore a string of kanji characters—the names and addresses of favored clients of hers, she said.

Tetsuko took a small brush and obliged. These names were far more important to Takenoha than the names of any flowers she might mention in love letters.

Mokusuke, farmer, Tadokoro village
Inejiro, cooper, Kinkei-cho
Kineji, yeast brewer, Tachibana village
Izo, blacksmith, Toragatani

Ichi couldn't understand why the teacher didn't scold Takenoha for not paying attention in class.

"We're off to the bath!"

The new girls ran outside, each carrying a thin towel and a cloth bag filled with rice bran. After school, they had until dinner to take their bath. Every brothel had its own bath, with the oiran first to enter, followed by the other courtesans in descending order of rank.

Prostitutes at the bottom, like Ichi and her companions, went to the big public bath in the licensed quarter.

They undressed and opened the door to the steamy washing area. Inside, the pale bodies of naked women were everywhere, a sight that Ichi always found startling. On her island there were no public baths.

When Ichi's mother and older sister emerged from the sea, they, too, were generally naked except for a loincloth, but this nudity was different. These women, although mostly younger than her mother and sister, had no muscles to speak of. Their bodies were voluptuous, plump, soft, and white. Some of the older women were pallid and flabby, others pitifully skinny, with prominent bones and tendons.

One woman's posterior caught Ichi's eyes. On each bony haunch was a hard-looking knob. Ichi nudged Kikumaru, beside her, and motioned silently to the woman. Kikumaru nodded.

"Knobby backside," she whispered. The result of lying pinned under a straddling man, pressed hard into the futon by his weight as your hips rolled about. Over time, this repetitive action caused the formation of knobs as hard as wood. Ichi had never seen anything like it.

The woman was pale and wan, but she didn't seem very old. As she began to wash her back, she turned her head and saw Ichi.

"Hey," Ichi said in surprise.

Takenoha broke into a smile. "Haven't seen you in a while."

She hadn't been back to school since that day. After she stopped coming, Ichi had worried. "Didja stay away 'cause I snitched on you to the teacher?"

Takenoha shook her head. "No, I've been working. Decided I'll go back home to my folks next year." She reached out with a big smile and laid a cautious hand on Ichi's firm, supple arm. "Such nice skin you've got! I'll wash your back for you. You remind me of my baby sis." She scrubbed Ichi's back with a soapy cloth. "Soft as a newborn calf."

When Ichi tried to return the favor, Takenoha protested and turned to hide her knobby backside. "No, it's okay. I already washed myself."

After that Takenoha lingered, soaking in the hot tub and showing no inclination to get dressed. Kikumaru, Kogin, and the rest were due to take their places on display behind the storefront lattice, so they left.

Finally, Takenoha went into a corner of the changing room and got dressed facing the wall. Her underskirt was faded from many washings and the knobs on her backside had worn through the material, exposing the skin beneath. Ichi averted her eyes and put on her own kimono.

Ichi and Takenoha left the bathhouse together. The sun was slanting low in the sky, but today for some reason Takenoha was in no hurry.

"You got enough time to get yourself ready?" Ichi asked.

"Yep. My customer's not due till after nine tonight. That's why I could have a nice long soak for a change."

Their bare feet were stuck into geta clogs that clattered on the pavement as they walked along.

"What about you? Don't you have to hurry?"

"No, I'm still an attendant in my oiran's room. I'm not even a beginner yet."

"That's good. That's really good." Takenoha repeated the words half to herself.

White puffs of smoke wafted from the bathhouse chimney into the somewhat overcast evening sky. Ichi was reminded of the smoke of the volcano back home.

"The chimney smoke reminds me of home," she said. The picture was so vivid in her mind's eye she could almost reach out and touch it.

"Yeah? Where's home?"

"An island south of Satsuma. It's got a volcano that spits fire."

Takenoha's voice lit up. "I'm from Kumamoto. The house I was born in is at the foot of Mount Aso. Mount Aso spits fire, too. It's a great big fiery volcano."

Ichi had never heard of that volcano, and Takenoha had never heard of Iojima. Neither of them knew much about the world.

"Whenever I see smoke, I remember sea turtles back home—giant ones that swim in the sea around our island. They're like gods," Ichi said with pride.

"When *I* see the smoke," said Takenoha, "I remember cows. My folks raise cattle in a pasture at the foot of the volcano. It's been more than ten years since I left. In the wintertime, a cow's horns are warm. When my hands got cold, I'd hug a cow's head for warmth."

Takenoha held out her thin arms and, using the hand towel, demonstrated how she used to hug a cow. She waved goodbye in front of the Kagetsu.

Ichi never saw Takenoha again.

Maybe she was still busy with work? Ichi looked for her in vain every day at the bath.

At school she asked the teacher if she knew where Takenoha was. Without even a flicker of an eyebrow, Tetsuko replied quietly as she corrected Ichi's characters with red ink: "I wonder. Perhaps she has gone somewhere far away. She came here from Osaka, so perhaps she has moved on to someplace new."

"And far away? Like where?"

"Up north, maybe, where there are fishing grounds and lots of brothels."

Ichi could not envision a northern city. She had never seen snow.

Laying down her brush, Tetsuko murmured, "Wherever she may be, I am sure she is working hard."

"Goodbye, teacher!" the girls said in chorus, and stood up, cloth bundles in hand.

"Goodbye," Tetsuko answered.

Their footsteps disappeared down the hall.

Alone, Tetsuko looked out the window for a while, then opened her desk drawer and gently removed something wrapped in a shabby cloth. It was a notebook, the very one containing Takenoha's record of her work. The pages were packed with writing in a cramped, clumsy hand.

July 4

Saw off Takichi. 1 p.m.–5 p.m., Kansuke, carpenter, Fujiidera-cho, 55 sen.

7 p.m.–10 a.m., Kinosuke, Kisaragi-cho, 1 yen 40 sen.

July 5

Saw off Kinosuke. 3 p.m.–5 p.m. Sakuzo, plasterer, Tatemachi, 30 sen. 8 p.m.–10 p.m., Chobei, Mitsuse village, 60 sen.

July 6

10 a.m.–2 p.m. Kurokichi, horse trader, Tomihisa

village, 25 sen. 9:30 p.m.–7 a.m., Kingo, carpenter, Kurokami-cho, 2 yen 20 sen.

July 7
Saw off Kingo. 11 a.m.–3 p.m., Hisagoro, gardener, Minatogawa-cho, 60 sen.

7 p.m. Takichi, carpenter, Sakae-cho. He came but I was ill. My chest hurt. Takichi left 20 sen and went away. I had a fever in the night.

July 8
Ill today. Doctor came. Cost 8 sen 50 rin.

July 9
Ill today. Doctor came again. Cost 12 sen.

The record stopped there; the rest was blank.

Tetsuko leafed back through the pages, counting on her fingers. In the eight days before she collapsed, Takenoha had received seventeen clients, counting the last one, Takichi. Tetsuko let out a deep sigh. She started to calculate how much Takenoha had earned before she died, but she stopped herself.

Takenoha's family would see to that. All she could do for the dead woman now was to make sure that this notebook went to her family.

The Ants Wept

Ichi was polishing a long hallway in the Shinonome, her head down and her rear end high in the air. A retired lumber dealer well into his eighties watched as she flew down the length of the hallway all the way to the toilet, kicking her feet up behind her. In front of the toilet she turned around, changed the direction of her cleaning cloth, and came charging back like a young wild boar.

The soles of her feet flashed. For such a young thing she had a nicely arched foot. The old man stared at her flying feet. The island girl was tireless. She'd gone up and down the hallway any number of times now without losing steam. She was a ball of fire. When she set out to clean a floor, she did it with her whole heart.

Early in September, the old man asked to spend the night with Ichi. Since she hadn't sat behind the lattice yet, Hajima Mohei was surprised. He explained that Ichi was only fifteen, but the old man pointed out that at the

New Year she would be sixteen and that he had been a loyal customer for many years.

"My girls don't start work until they're seventeen," said Mohei.

"I won't touch her. I just want to sleep beside her and hold her." The old man's heart was set on spending the night with Ichi.

When it came time for one of his girls to begin work, Mohei would first talk to her and prepare her for what lay ahead. Ichi wasn't ready. Her speech was still unrefined and she was capable of physical violence. Remembering the time she'd flattened Shinonome with a kick, Mohei pondered what to do.

A few days later, Mohei informed Ichi that a very important elderly client had requested her company for the night. She listened quietly as he laid out dos and don'ts: Whatever the old man did, she must not show displeasure or interfere in any way. She must not address him familiarly. Better yet, she should keep her mouth shut. All she needed to do was nod. She must behave just as Shinonome had taught her, walking slowly with her toes turned in and not gobbling food and drink even if it was offered.

Ichi left Mohei's room and found Shinonome waiting for her upstairs, along with Murasaki. She felt a twinge of alarm, but it was too late. The fusuma doors to an adjoining room clattered open and a pair of manservants named Muraji and Shinzo—burly fellows who stood watch and did odd jobs—each grabbed her by an arm, then shoved her down on her back and pushed up the skirt of her kimono. Ichi screamed and thrashed her legs as they held her pinned, one on either side.

Shinonome gave a twittering laugh. "You're not going to be murdered. You're going to receive your first customer. You simply cannot let him see all that unsightly hair."

Small tweezers gleamed in the hands of Shinonome and Murasaki. The men pried Ichi's legs apart, and the tweezers set to work. With each pluck, Ichi's hips shivered.

"Ow, ow! I'll be ashamed with no hair down there!"

"Just look! You were shaggy and now you're nice and smooth. Hair is like weeds that spoil the scenery: it has to go."

Ichi went on yelling bloody murder. Attracted by the commotion, people came up the stairs with much trepidation and cautiously slid open the door. They gaped at the scene inside, with Ichi flailing wildly. The men were on the verge of giving her a thrashing, when Mohei stopped them. If she were injured now, he would suffer a tremendous loss.

The main thing was to present Ichi to the old man. For a young prostitute's debut, an octogenarian was ideal.

That he had volunteered for the role without prompting or pressure was a piece of great good fortune. If her first client didn't hurry or force himself on her but rather cherished her, the memory would be a beacon across life's sea of suffering. An old man was a rich blessing. How could they make her understand?

Tweezers in hand, Shinonome raised her head.

That was enough for today. If they pulled out all her pubic hair at once, the skin would be red and swollen. Best to do a little at a time. She would ask the men back again tomorrow. She and Murasaki heaved sighs of exhaustion, and the onlookers drifted back downstairs. Ichi sat up on the tatami, her hair in disarray and her face flushed red, and looked down at her crotch—oddly patchy now, like a partially weeded field.

That evening, as Murasaki leaned against her window frame, she spotted Ichi crouched in the garden below. "What are you doing?" she called.

"Looking at ants." Ichi picked one up with her fingers and held it up for Murasaki to see. "They're teeny, but they each have a little face. I'm making friends with them."

Murasaki smiled, thinking what an odd child she was.

The "weeding" took three days.

Shinonome next turned her attention upward and shaved off Ichi's fine, downy facial hair. Then she shaped

Ichi's eyebrows into slender arches. That alone transformed the girl's appearance, making her look much more feminine.

"Now walk," Shinonome ordered, seated with a long-stemmed pipe in hand. When Ichi started out with long strides like a man, Shinonome smacked her on the leg with her pipe.

"Owww!" Ichi grimaced in pain.

"Tighten your thigh muscles and walk pigeon-toed."

Ichi tried again.

"Good. Now come sit over here."

Ichi obediently went over and plopped down beside her.

"Look at me."

As Ichi turned her head with a vacant look, mouth half-open, Shinonome reached out and gave her face a hard pinch.

"Owww!"

Ignoring Ichi's grimace of pain, Shinonome went over to a set of silk futons laid out in a corner of the room and knelt by the pillows.

"Kojika, come here and get in."

It was the sumptuous bedding of eye-popping scarlet used only by oirans. Ichi was too dazed to move.

"Come on," Shinonome said, beckoning.

Murasaki was grinning. Ichi moved awkwardly across the room, her body tense.

"Watch now. This is how you invite a client in."

Holding the quilt at the top, she folded it back crosswise and gently laid the "client"—Ichi—down. Then, seated gracefully at the edge of the futon with her legs to one side, she turned her back to the client. Raising a hand, she pulled out the ornamental hairpins in her chignon. The curve of her back, visible through the thin silk of her underkimono, was like the crescent moon. After allowing the client's eyes to feast on this view, she slid sideways onto the futon, starting with her right shoulder.

Shinonome and Ichi lay face-to-face under the quilt, their bosoms inches apart. The fragrance and heat of Shinonome's body enveloped Ichi. Spellbound, she half closed her eyes. Shinonome's body was warm for one so slender.

Ma, Ichi thought, and shut her eyes, once again a child sleeping nestled by its mother. Shinonome was transformed.

Breathing in Ichi's ear, Shinonome said: "Listen well. You mustn't let a client do as he pleases with your body. Our bodies are our greatest possession. They are precious. Instead of having a client touch us, we touch him. And little by little, we lead him to paradise." One arm encircled Ichi's shoulders as the other slid toward the front of her kimono. "But your client tomorrow is an old man who no longer wants paradise in this life.

Instead, he will take *you* there. Let him have his way. Do you follow me?"

Shinonome's hand didn't seem to be a hand. It was a small, lukewarm fish. With a shake of its tail, the little fish came gliding up from the hem of Ichi's kimono in search of the path to water and, wriggling its tiny, finger-size body, burrowed its way in. Overlaying this was Shinonome's voice: "Listen well. This isn't my hand, it's the hand of old Mr. Totsuka."

Ichi gulped and then gasped for breath, drowning. Her arms no longer lay limp. She reached out frantically and clutched Shinonome's sides. She made a sputtering noise, as if her head were half-underwater.

"Tighten your throat. Don't make such ugly sounds—you'll spoil the mood. A woman's voice should sound delicate."

"Ahhh."

"Yes. Perfect."

Ichi was utterly compliant. Murasaki stood up and left the room with a look that said, *Whew, that's a relief.*

"Ahhh."

"That's the way. Good girl." Shinonome put her lips to Ichi's sweat-soaked forehead. "Good girl." She got up, leaving Ichi alone on the futon like a stranded fish.

"Kojika."

Ichi opened her eyes and looked at Shinonome in a stupor.

"Listen well. If you conduct yourself this way, he will come again to see you. You understand, don't you?"

Ichi nodded. Her eyes were glazed, like those of someone delirious with fever. In all her fifteen years, never had she felt anything so wonderful. Then again, were the sensations she had felt wonderful or terrible? She didn't know. Eddies of pleasure and pain had coursed through her again and again. As the maelstrom intensified, her body had floated upward.

Shinonome's powers were extraordinary.

Ichi had a client.

Mr. Totsuka, the retired lumber dealer, came to see her night after night. This was unheard of. Everyone was as surprised as if cherry blossoms had bloomed on the bamboo fence out back. Ichi was untrained in the arts and still ran noisily down the hallway, like a boy.

Each night, the old gentleman summoned manservants and prostitutes who had failed to attract clients for the evening, treated them to sake, and had them dance and enjoy themselves. Soon after nine o'clock, he retired to a bedroom with Ichi. "No accounting for taste," people murmured.

The news reached Tetsuko, upsetting her. How could Hajima Mohei have permitted this to happen? Ichi was too young to take clients. Even granting that this client was an old man, the fact remained that Ichi had now gone into the business of prostitution.

But Ichi kept coming to school, wearing the same short kimono of coarse cotton and straw sandals with stretched-out thongs. Kogin, Kikumaru, and the rest were oddly quiet, since Ichi, though still underage, had somehow snagged a steady client before them.

Docile now, Ichi plied her brush.

September 10 Aoi Ichi

Yesterday Hidemaru wore a summer kimono.
It made me think of *kamimairi* on the island.
The older boys and girls would stream out at
  night
wearing cotton kimonos.
Where they went and what they did I never
  knew
but these days I have some idea.
Couples went into the grass in the dark.

"Kamimairi?" asked Tetsuko, looking at what Ichi had written in her usual clumsy scrawl.

"You never heard of it?"

Ichi tried to explain, but Tetsuko couldn't understand her dialect.

Couples went into the grass in the dark. It sounded like

lovers' trysts, she thought, but since they "streamed out," they must do it en masse. Perhaps this was some sort of village fertility ritual like those she had read about in old books. Apparently such goings-on were a tradition on Ichi's home island.

Tetsuko looked silently at Ichi's face. Ichi was smiling ever so slightly and nodding. The girl from the southern island had never had such a look in her eyes before. She was smiling with her mouth half-open.

September 11 Aoi Ichi

Last night a customer came, an old man.
Everybody soon gathered and there was plenty of sake and food.
After we ate we went into the bedroom and went to bed.
"Shall we go to paradise?" he said.
An old mans paradise is sleep.
He will be in paradise for real soon enough.

"Your customers," Tetsuko said, including Kogin, Kikumaru, and the rest in her gaze, "should never appear in your writing. You must never talk about them with others, either. What happens between a customer and you is for only the two of you to know. It is confidential, something you share with him alone."

Ichi lowered her head. She looked unsatisfied.

"If you wrote every thought in your mind, nobody could live in peace anymore. Aoi Ichi, how would you feel if your client wrote about you?"

Ichi understood.

After the students had all left, Tetsuko took out Ichi's essay and reread it. The retired Mr. Totsuka was apparently gentle with Ichi. But there was no way of knowing what he did with her body. Was this wealthy old man content at the end of his life merely to admire the beauty of a wildflower as yet unplucked? Or had Ichi already taken on the role of prostitute, at age fifteen?

Ichi's slight smile rose before her eyes. Ichi had remembered here the custom on her home island of illicit mingling between the sexes—kamimairi, or whatever it was called. To Tetsuko, who had grown up in the city, such a thing was inconceivable, but perhaps in remote villages young people did indulge in licentious diversions in the dark of night. If it were true, what barbarism!

When she was on the island, Ichi had not understood what the custom involved, but now she did. Hence the smile.

The youngest girl in the batch of new arrivals that spring had caught up with and surpassed her colleagues, determined not to be outdone. Perhaps she was better off smiling than weeping and being miserable, yet Tetsuko had a lump in her throat. She was remembering the stormy days she herself had endured after being sold to that Yoshiwara brothel long ago.

Even now, the memories stung.

After the Meiji Restoration, when Edo was renamed Tokyo, low-ranking, low-paid samurai of the Tokugawa shogunate like her father had lost their livelihoods. Many of them began relocating to Shizuoka to open tea plantations, but her father couldn't afford to transport his family of eleven, including his wife, parents, and seven children. Tetsuko, the eldest, had been sacrificed to save them all from penury. He came to her secretly and begged. Her mother, whose family ranked higher than his, never knew.

"I will be tutoring the daughters of a rich merchant," Tetsuko had assured her weeping mother, clutching her by the hands and promising to rejoin the family soon.

Many daughters of samurais had shared her fate.

When the Yoshiwara brothel owner first laid eyes on her, he had sighed and said, "This one'll take up a lot of space in bed."

She was as tall as a man. Her eyes were narrow, her lips thin. Though not homely, she had failed to win over her customers because she made no effort to please them. Rather, she had put them off. She could never understand why human beings had to be divided into those who bought others and those who were sold.

As the daughter of a samurai, she had considerable

pride and would talk back even to the brothel owner, answering a word of reproof with a dozen arguments. She nicknamed the owner Mohachi ("lacking eight"), for he possessed none of the eight traditional virtues: benevolence, righteousness, propriety, integrity, trust, loyalty, filial piety, and respect for elders.

This vile man had bought her, and she must sell herself to vile customers to stay alive. Oh, the humiliation! Oh, her womanly purity! The word "virginity" was unfamiliar to her, but the word "chastity" seared her heart.

She and the other girls encouraged each other: "Even though our bodies are sinking now beneath the waves, let's keep our spirits aiming high."

The average age of retirement for prostitutes was twenty-seven. Ten years after making their debut, they were finally free to leave. Even then, some of them were enmeshed in darkness, sinking of their own accord to steadily more disreputable brothels. Tetsuko sought a decent life. She took any job: bookkeeper in the licensed quarter, seamstress, assistant midwife.

The treatise *New Greater Learning for Women* by Fukuzawa Yukichi had begun appearing in the journal *Jiji Shimpo* in 1899, and its contents thawed Tetsuko's frozen heart like sunshine streaming through clouds. It was as if the original *Greater Learning for Women*, imbued with old-fashioned Confucian values, had grown wings and taken flight. She read passages such as this with a thrill:

> When girls have gotten a bit older, they should have physical education just like boys, and as long as they don't injure themselves, they should be allowed to enjoy rough sports, too.

She also liked the part where Yukichi urged the study of new subjects:

> When it comes to learning, there is no difference between boys and girls. Both sexes should study physics as the basis of learning, and from there branch out to other subjects.

Women and physics. What a fresh and beautiful combination! Tetsuko was entranced.

Yukichi went on to write that no subject, apart from military science, was useless for women to study. Tetsuko devoutly wished she had been born in this new age, not in feudal times. Or that she could raise a daughter of her own in these exciting times. But she was single, so that wish, too, could not be fulfilled.

She thought of other living things. Plants could blossom and bear fruit on their own; why couldn't a female animal bear young unaided?

One other passage in *New Greater Learning for Women* made her want to shout for joy. Yukichi pointed out that feminine regard for beauty and elegance had led women to learn mainly creative arts such as music, tea ceremony, ikebana, poetry, haiku, and calligraphy; he warned against reading classical literature and poetry for pleasure, however, for although the words might be beautiful, the contents tended toward the obscene.

> *Hyakunin Isshu*, for example, is harmless for girls to read or listen to avidly, but commentary or translations into modern colloquial language would be lewd and scarcely worth listening to.

To Yukichi, all one hundred poets represented in the venerable anthology, including Emperor Tenji, Kakinomoto no Hitomaro, Murasaki Shikibu, and Sei Shonagon, were equally blameworthy. He disapproved of having women devote their lives to the study of such writers. Doing so, he declared, would only encourage them in frivolity and leave them ignorant of physics.

She had to agree that *Hyakunin Isshu* was certainly no place to learn basic concepts of physics. All in all, she was delighted.

The world was changing.

Though unable to give birth to a daughter of her own in this new age when one could state unequivocally that classical *waka* poems of thirty-one syllables were indecent, Tetsuko was determined at the very least to protect the minds of young prostitutes in her charge and keep them from becoming debauched.

In her mind's eye, she saw Ichi with that slight smile on her face.

The private bath in the Shinonome brothel had a large cypress tub that overnight clients used, together with oirans and other high-ranking courtesans, before they left in the early morning. Last night there had been no overnight guests, so Shinonome was enjoying a leisurely bath, breathing in the fragrance of cypress while she washed her lustrous skin.

Ichi was there, too, to wash the oiran's back.

When they washed themselves on Ichi's home island, they set a wooden tub on the beach, filled it with water, and heated it over a driftwood fire. The women's bodies were tanned bronze, front and back. Shinonome's skin, on the other hand, was the soft white of flower petals. She carefully washed herself not with soap but with a soft cloth bag filled with rice bran and nightingale droppings.

The licensed quarter naturally lavished care on its clientele, but owners reserved their greatest consideration for oirans. Ichi found this odd, since the oirans were after all prostitutes, too. But the owners spoke to them with utmost deference. Oirans were served special meals and reigned like empresses.

Each empress was capable of supporting more than a hundred ordinary prostitutes. The Shinonome empresses underwrote the expenses of everyone from young servants to manservants, cooks, laundresses, and kamuros, little girls who waited on oirans, all the way up to Mohei, who controlled the Osaka rice market: the oirans supported them all.

There were presently three oirans in the local licensed quarter, two of whom, Shinonome and Murasaki, belonged to the Shinonome brothel. Ichi was now washing the back of one of those empresses. The hue and delicacy of her skin were incomparable. Ichi resembled her in one aspect only: neither of them had any hair down below. Morning light streaming through the window lit up their smooth private parts.

"How is Mr. Totsuka these days?" Shinonome asked.

"Well, he's . . . he doesn't do anything," Ichi said. He must feel like he was sleeping with his arms around his granddaughter, she thought. When she awoke in the middle of the night, she would be spread-eagled in the middle of the futon, and he would be huddled at the edge like a withered tree. The gold-painted Satsuma-ware jar containing his false teeth cast a lonely shadow.

"That's a bit of a shame, isn't it?" Shinonome washed an ear.

"Yep. If he's going to pay money, he ought to do what he's supposed to do. This way, I feel uncomfortable."

"Oh my. Sounds as if someone is good and ready."

Ichi smiled. "Yep, the thought doesn't bother me at all!"

"You surprise me."

"Really, it's nothing. All the young men and women do it. On the night of kamimairi, everyone is intimate with someone. Even my folks."

Shinonome's laughter echoed in the bath. "Your father and mother?"

"Yep."

Shinonome was from Kyoto, a city girl. After her father's weaving business went under, she had entered the licensed quarter of Shimabara at age ten as a kamuro, a future oiran. People in the city formed professional guilds, but there was no strong bond among them. They tended to associate only with their immediate neighbors.

In the countryside, farming or fishing villages formed a unit like an extended family. A single granary sufficed for the entire village. Children, the next generation of workers, were a community asset. During busy seasons for fishing or farming, villagers took turns watching, feeding, and looking after them. Wives and daughters also belonged to the village as a whole. It didn't happen often, but on moonlit nights in the tenth lunar month, when all the Shinto gods were off at Izumo

Shrine, islanders would seize the opportunity to couple off and make love.

"Making love in the moonlight sounds rather charming."

"After that, cute little babies are born all over the island." Ichi pretended to rock an infant in her arms.

Moonlight on the bare arms and legs of people crawling through grasses: the image flashed through Shinonome's mind. She recalled the expression *yago*, "rustic encounter." For a moment she was repelled by what seemed a sordid custom, but she was forced to admit that the system of total strangers buying and selling intimacy was little better.

"Doesn't bother me," Ichi repeated. "It's all right."

Shinonome glanced at Ichi's crotch, innocently on display. Her hairless sex gave the impression of a closed eyelid. The eyelid between Shinonome's own legs was soft and fleshy, ever ready to open. Ichi's was sealed tightly shut. Inside her was a girl still unexposed to the world.

It was October on the island of Kyushu.

Summer's scorching heat was gone, and signs of autumn had set in.

One morning, there was a disturbance at the brothel. All-night customers normally left at four in the morning, before the sun rose. That night there were five all-night customers, including Shinonome's client. Care was taken to stagger departure times so the five wouldn't run into one another as they left. When the last one, old Mr. Totsuka, finally appeared, those gathered to see him off were rendered speechless with shock.

The old man's face was swollen and purple from his eyelids to his nose. He looked completely different than when he arrived. He didn't utter a word. Ichi came to see him off, frowning and silent. The others stood around, rattled, with no idea what to say. Finally his rickshaw came and bore him away.

Word was quickly sent to Mohei, and he and Tose came running. Mohei remembered the time Ichi had kicked Shinonome and Murasaki.

There was no need to ask what had happened.

As before, Ichi was bound to a pillar in the kitchen, sitting with her legs to one side. Mohei kicked her hard in the thigh. "What did you do to your customer? Here's what you did! You punched an old man right in the face!"

This time he let her have it in the face. Her flesh rang. She wailed in pain.

After boxing her once more on the cheek, Mohei went and changed his kimono, put on a silk haori, and called for a palanquin. He had to go to the Totsuka home to offer his apologies. How many times he might need to prostrate himself in abject contrition, he had no idea.

That night, Ichi slept tied to the pillar.

Sometime in the night, she awoke from the pain of the rope cutting into her arms to find Shinonome standing in front of her, holding a cup of water.

"Here," Shinonome said, holding the cup to Ichi's lips. "You must be thirsty."

Ichi gulped greedily.

"I brought you a rice ball, too."

Ichi devoured it. Her mouth was split open, but that didn't slow her down.

Shinonome looked down at her with pity. "Why didn't you like the old man? I thought you were prepared to sleep with anyone without complaining."

Rice grains were stuck around the outside of Ichi's mouth. "Not with a geezer," she said.

"What?"

"I hate geezers."

"Why, you little . . ." Shinonome clucked her tongue. Who did Kojika think she was? It wasn't her place to be particular! Without a second thought she slapped Ichi's face and left.

No matter how many times she was punched and slapped, Ichi wouldn't stay away from the Female Industrial School. So far, she had perfect attendance.

The next day, she went to school with a swollen face and wrote these sentences.

October 20 Aoi Ichi

Recently I made friends with ants.
On the ground in the garden
I tell them many things.
Theres so much I want to say
but I dont tell them secrets.
I dont tell anyone.
Its true.

Tetsuko corrected the shape of Ichi's letters with red ink, folded the paper in two, and tucked it away in her desk drawer.

The Ground Fell Away

After lunch, as Ichi was getting ready for school, the brothel manager, Saito, called her from the foot of the stairs.

"The master has something important to say to you, so come to the office."

"I'm going to school."

"What he has to say is more important."

Come to think of it, Saito rarely said a word to Ichi. He spent all his time in the office and never dealt with any females except Tose and old Otoku. Ichi had never spoken to him before, but she had heard other girls say his name.

When Ichi went downstairs, she found Hajima Mohei, Tose, and Shinonome seated in the office. She presented herself fearfully, and Saito said in a cold voice: "Kojika. Your oiran tells us that your monthlies started some time ago. Is that true?"

"Yep." She nodded. The bodies of island girls, toned

by the sea, developed quickly. Ichi had been sold here in the spring, soon after her first menstrual period.

"I see. In that case, I advise you to pay close attention to what the master says."

Mohei took over. "Kojika. A prostitute's initiation normally comes after she turns seventeen, but those who wish to begin repaying their debt sooner may start as soon as their monthlies begin. Do you want to start now?"

"Yep." She nodded again.

The master's words were forceful, allowing no dissent. The word "initiation" had a sinister ring. She had overheard Kogin, Kikumaru, and Hanaji whisper it among themselves. This was the threshold that younger girls must eventually cross. One after another, each of them had taken her first customer and opened her body to him.

"Very well. Then your initiation starts this month."

Ichi thought of the recent uproar with old Mr. Totsuka. That had been the prologue. This time there would be no escape. Disqualified by her behavior from ever becoming an oiran, she must now get busy earning her keep.

"From now on you'll work. Earn a living with your body and pay off your debt little by little. And remember: pull any stunts like the other day, and you'll get no food. Whether your life here is hell on earth or paradise is up to you. Is that clear?"

Ichi's shoulders were hunched. Was she listening or not? Mohei could never tell.

"Yep." She nodded, cowed into submission.

"Paradise" must refer to Shinonome's lifestyle, settled as she was in a luxurious apartment while all around more than a hundred other courtesans jostled for space. Ichi had yet to glimpse hell.

Tose looked at Shinonome and then said to Ichi, "The oiran here will see to all the necessary preparations, from your underkimono to your kimono and sash. Don't forget how much you owe her, and conduct yourself as you should."

Ichi looked innocently bewildered.

"You must do your best!" Shinonome flashed her a brilliant smile.

Back at Shinonome's apartment, Ichi's new kimono and accessories were laid out for her. Otoku motioned to Ichi to come closer and helped her put on a red underkimono.

The garments were all bright red, the color worn by little girls, since an initiate was still a child. The red kimono with flowing sleeves always had the same design, the celestial robe of feathers. Shinonome initiates were also issued a woven sash, tabi socks, and hair ornaments, none of which came cheaply. If there was no one to cover the cost, it was of course added on to each girl's debt.

Each oiran saw to the needs of the kamuro who waited on her and also oversaw the education of girls like Ichi, paying all their expenses out of her earnings. Tight-fisted women were not cut out to be oirans.

"You know what they say," said Otoku. "Fine clothes make even a monkey look fine."

"You mean a horse driver, not a monkey," corrected Shinonome.

"Oh, is that how it goes?" Otoku cackled. Looking at Ichi, she still thought her version was more apt.

Ichi held the clothes in her arms and rubbed her cheek against the silk. "So, so beautiful!" she burst out in island dialect.

"Hey! I told you, we don't understand your bird talk here!" Otoku's long-stemmed pipe smacked Ichi across the bottom. "Tell the oiran how grateful you are."

Ichi fidgeted and stammered, "Oiran, thank you, very much."

The monkey child had apparently mastered a bit of human speech after all.

Early in the evening, as the lanterns were lit behind the wooden lattice and the strains of the shamisen sounded, Ichi went out to sit with the others, the skirt of her kimono trailing behind her. Her face had been so carefully made up by Shinonome that she was almost unrecognizable. Only oirans were exempt from sitting on display. The profusion of women was like a hundred flowers blossoming together in the lantern light. Ichi sat among them in her red kimono with flowing sleeves. But on the night of her debut and again the following night, no one picked her. Though there was no shortage of customers, no one lingered in front of Ichi.

Ichi stopped going to school, not wanting to show her face. "I'm so ashamed. Why doesn't anyone pick me?"

Tamagiku, the kamuro attending to Shinonome, was ten years old. "It's because you're always staring at the customers."

"I can't look at them?"

"It's the customers who look over the girls."

Of course. "Then what do I do?"

"Just stare at the end of your nose."

What a funny thing to say. "Like this?" Ichi went cross-eyed.

"No, silly. Just sit quietly and mind your own business. Try to look like Kannon, the goddess of mercy, the way Shinonome does. See? Like this." Tamagiku stared at a point in space. She did resemble Shinonome a bit.

Kamuros wore their hair shoulder length, clipped neatly all the way around, and always dressed in a kimono with flowing sleeves. They didn't pour sake for customers and never spoke or flirted but just stuck quietly to the oiran's side. Though children, they were future candidates for the position of oiran and came generally from good families that had fallen on hard times. They had fine features and a bent for learning, making communication difficult with unlettered girls from rural villages like Ichi.

"That's what Kannon looks like?"

"Yes. Men adore Kannon. That's why they come to the licensed quarter, to worship her. That's what the oiran said." Tamagiku's face was like a small lily. "So I'm going to become a Kannon."

"I could never do that," Ichi murmured in sorrow.

The peach-blossom class was practicing writing one afternoon. As they finished one sheet, they solemnly read over the lines they had written. Some then started over; others picked up their paper and took it to Tetsuko, seated at her desk, for her to check.

"When you are finished, you may leave," said Tetsuko.

One, then two, then three girls bowed and left the classroom.

Tetsuko went over to Ichi's desk. "You are writing quite a lot today!"

Ichi handed in two sheets of paper, then picked up her brush and went on writing. Or no, not writing, thinking. As she pondered, words arose in her mind and aligned themselves on the page.

Tetsuko went back to her desk by the window and spread out the pages Ichi had written.

November 18 Aoi Ichi

I got a red kimono.
Every night I put it on and sit out front.
Its made of smooth soft silk from silkworms.
The skin of an oirans face is like silk.
The skin of my mas face is like hemp.
The skin of my little sisters face is like cotton.
The skin of my grannys face is like banana
fabric.
To be honest my face is cotton.
Thats why Ive got no takers.

Tetsuko had grown fairly used to Ichi's dialect. At once funny and poignant—that was Ichi's journal.

Tetsuko studied Ichi's no-longer-suntanned face. Yes, she could see it: Ichi had skin like tightly woven, sturdy cotton. Even cotton cloth had luster, but it lacked the sleekness of silk. Silk was too shiny. Her own skin was probably cotton, too, like Ichi's. But she, Tetsuko, was no longer a prostitute, while Ichi was a girl forced to sell herself. Tetsuko's heart ached.

November 18, continued Aoi Ichi

Theres something strange.
The doctor who comes to Female Industrial
School says
initiation means you stop being a virgin

but the oiran says
Ill keep wearing the red kimono
3 months 4 months even 6 months more
Suppose Im sold 3 times?
2 will be a lie
If Im sold 5 times
4 will be a lie
If Im sold 10 times
9 will be a lie
And if as many as 30 times in 6 months
29 will be a lie
How awful!

Ichi bent over her paper. Tetsuko sat with her elbows propped on her desktop and wondered what to do. Ichi seemed ready to go on writing forever.

"Aoi Ichi."

"Yes'm."

"It is time you headed to the bath. The sun is going down."

When it grew dark, the shamisen music started up and the show began. The boisterous twanging kept up until after midnight, closing time, while behind the lattice, prostitutes awaited customers. For as long as the music played, women of pleasure must gyrate on scarlet futons.

Ichi came to herself and started to gather up her writing things.

Tetsuko buried the embers in the hibachi beneath the ashes.

"It's better not to know anything," said Shinonome. "Just follow the client's lead."

The oiran was responsible for offering those under her wing guidance concerning their first sexual experience. But no special technique was involved. All one had to do was weep and protest and the customer would be satisfied. The six months would pass quickly.

The manager Saito pulled some strings, and after four or five days first one customer, then another, came by to view Ichi. "There's a new flower ready for the plucking," he whispered in the ears of certain long-standing customers.

First-time customers were not allowed to sleep with girls having their first experience. Some men wanted to be informed whenever a young girl was making her debut. They were skilled in handling virgins and could be trusted. Moreover, they understood the workings of the house and would never complain, "That was no virgin!" Girls from the countryside had often been exposed to the tradition of "night crawling"—stealing into a woman's bedroom to make love—or had frequented "youth inns." Actual virgins were rare.

The night of November 20, 1903, was rather warm for the time of year.

The first customer Saito found was a man named Takahata who ran a pharmacy in town. He was a tall, big-boned man in his fifties who gave off the faintly acrid smell of medicinal herbs. Ichi knew him by sight, as he was a regular at the Shinonome.

Food and sake were set out for them on low tables, and farther inside the room was a scarlet futon. It was all just as it had been with old Mr. Totsuka. The meal, the sake, and the bedding were luxurious, in keeping with the client's high rank. For such a client, the fee for a deflowering, which required the girl only to weep in protest or, at most, to lie stiffly like a doll, was considerable.

But Ichi knew none of this. Having been instructed to say nothing, she kept her lips tightly closed as she poured Takahata a drink.

"You're called Kojika?"

She nodded.

"Where are you from?"

Ichi hung her head.

Raising the sake cup to his mouth, Takahata said, "Relax. I initiated every woman in this place. There's nothing to fear."

He then took the bottle and poured Ichi a drink. "Drink a little, you'll feel better."

Ichi accepted the cup in both hands and swallowed the sake.

"Where's your home?"

"Iojima."

"Ah. South of Satsuma. You've come a long way."

He poured her another drink. "Now you pour one for me."

She did so.

They emptied their cups.

"I'm not a great lover of women. But there's something endearing about a woman's first time. I love a woman on her first night. That's all."

Ichi felt strange, hearing herself referred to repeatedly as a woman. Until now she had always been called a girl.

"What makes a woman different from a girl?" she asked.

"A woman has known a man. A girl hasn't."

Takahata made it sound simple.

"You want to be a woman?"

She found herself nodding.

With old Mr. Totsuka, she'd been terrified to make the leap. The unfathomable shadows below had seemed to writhe with monsters, snakes, vipers, and evil spirits. Now the distance she must leap across felt empty. This man seemed nice. He had none of the old geezer's creepiness.

"If you want to find out, come here."

Takahata held out a hand that smelled of geranium—a diarrhea remedy—and in response to his invitation Ichi got up. A memory of her late grandfather's broad chest came to her. This man frightened her, but he also made her feel somehow nostalgic. She lay down beside him, and he slipped off her clothes. He caressed her round buttocks, as fleshy as ripe southern fruit. Wherever he stroked her, her skin was smooth, polished by the sea.

"Mm. Your skin feels so good."

As his hands stroked her all over, Ichi felt as though the contours of her body—her back, waist, hips, chest, legs—were just now coming into being. She was being born. She stretched out her arms and legs, raised her stomach, closed her eyes.

Something hot and huge pushed between her legs, a thick, heavy baton of flesh. She resisted as it pushed deep inside her, almost to her throat. It hurt. Here there were no monsters or snakes or evil spirits, only lacerating pain. It hurt. It hurt so much.

Feeling trampled, Ichi opened her eyes. Tears ran down her face.

Normally Ichi came bounding noisily downstairs, stuck her feet in a pair of straw sandals, and rushed outside, but the next morning she descended the stairs as though all the air had leaked out of her, a deflated ball.

Saito stuck his head out of the office. "Kojika! There are no customers now, so go have a nice long soak in the bath."

Outside, a chilly breeze ruffled the skirt of her kimono. She was reminded of last spring, when she first came here. After her island, she'd been continually cold. With her sleeve pressed against her face, she headed for the bathhouse and along the way heard low voices coming from the shed where firewood was stored.

Going closer to investigate, she realized it was the sound of women singing. She peered inside the shed and saw Kikumaru, Kogin, and two others huddled among the stacks of firewood, each holding a sheet of paper in one hand and singing away. Nearby was a man in black Western-style clothes, one of the Dutchmen who sometimes appeared in this area. Nagasaki was just across the harbor, so foreigners were not all that rare. Ichi, however, was surprised, having never seen a foreigner before. This man's skin was as white as a silkworm cocoon, and he had curly red hair. His arms and legs were long, like a spider's.

"Gofried, this is Kojika," Kikumaru said to the man. "She's one of us."

"We're learning songs," Kogin told Ichi. "Songs praising God."

They all started singing again.

Come, let us walk to the kingdom of light
Led by the Lamb of God

Hallelujah hallelujah hallelujah
Amen

Ichi caught her breath. What a funny sort of song! She had never heard such a melody or such lyrics before.

"Let's sing together, shall we?" Kikumaru invited her.

Ichi squared her shoulders proudly. "I can sing a song about a turtle." Standing rock still, she burst into song in her barely comprehensible dialect.

Master Turtle, where are you off to?
I drank all day, got stumbling drunk
Drank so much, I'm dizzy as can be
Where'd the ocean go?
Dizzy as can be

Kikumaru corrected her. "I didn't say *kame*, turtle; I said *kamisama*, God."

"On my island, turtles are gods."

"Gofried, I'm sorry. She doesn't know anything about the world."

"It's all right. Let's tell the poor girl about Jesus."

The foreigner spoke with a startling accent. Jesus was apparently the name of his god. Kikumaru and the others must have started worshipping that god, too.

For Ichi, the sight of a huge turtle three feet long was enough to make her shiver in awe. Sea turtles had no fear of humans and were perfectly happy to swim alongside them. Sometimes while they swam, one of them would look Ichi in the eye and wink—a signal that meant "Come here." When she saw the big blue shadow of a sea turtle in the bright, radiant sea, Ichi felt she had seen the shadow of a god.

Big things aroused awe in her: a cloud floating on the sea like an island; the sun, half-sunk into the waves, slowly dissolving as evening came on. Nothing else made her feel like bringing her hands together in worship.

"Kojika started taking customers this month."

"Oh, dear God."

Gofried looked down at Ichi with eyes of pity. His eyes were the color of the southern sea, Ichi thought. They seemed full of tears.

"Sing with us," Kogin urged, but Ichi remembered she had to be back to sit in her red kimono.

"I'm going to the bath." She ran off without a backward glance.

Late in the afternoon after everyone else had gone home, Ichi arrived at school, took out a piece of paper, and began to write, bent over the desk. The building was silent. Only the brush in her hand moved across the page as if alive. After a while, she held up the paper and read over what she had written. She got unsteadily to her feet, laid the paper gently on Tetsuko's desk, and left quickly, like a gust of wind.

Tetsuko, who had been out cleaning the hallway, came back to the classroom and untied the cord tucking up her kimono sleeves. She started to walk past her desk and stopped.

November 22 Aoi Ichi
Lately its cold.
My friends the ants went away.
Instead of them Ill tell you, my teacher.
The night of my initiation
the ground fell away.
When my ma and my sister went out in the
    moonlight
I thought it looked fun.
I really thought it was something good.
The ground fell away beneath my feet.
Tomorrow how can I go on working?

Those moonlit adventures between island men and women that Ichi had once described to Tetsuko must have appeared thrilling in the eyes of a child.

The workings of the human heart were integral to the potential in sex for pain and pleasure, Tetsuko believed. Without the involvement of the intricate, rich world of the emotions, intercourse brought a woman only pain. To the fifteen-year-old who had found this out, “the ground fell away beneath my feet.” The sensation of a world without a foundation was something Tetsuko knew all too well. She knew it in her bones, in her very core: a world without solid footing, a world where one could move neither forward nor backward but only sink deeper with each effort, lost in body and mind. Tetsuko had endured the vicissitudes of that world, managing to survive until her contract expired when she was twenty-seven. By then disease had carried off more of her coworkers than she could count.

After that brief, unexpected visit, Ichi stopped coming to school. Even in the warm climate of southern Kyushu, there were days when shining bits of silvery ice danced in the air. On freezing evenings in the quarter, the lively twang of the shamisen resonated through the streets and the glow of lanterns banished the night. As Tetsuko locked up, she listened to the far-off strains.

Ten days had passed since Ichi had begun taking clients. She had already entertained four.

As the early winter sun went down, she sat behind the lattice, feeling the chill of the wind. A young man came down the street, dressed for travel and carrying a sack on his shoulders. Back and forth he went, searching the women’s faces. Though winter was coming on, he had the sunburned face of summer.

"Teriha. Teriha, are you there?" he called in a low voice.

Ichi gulped. She knew that dark, shining face. She crept closer to the lattice. "Shokkichi! I know you. You're the son of the island head."

The young man's eyes popped. "Who're you?"

"Aoi Ichi from Iojima."

"Gah! You're one of the Aoi sisters? What are you doing here?"

"I got sold, too. Just like one of the island cows."

Shokkichi was a cowherd traveling in Kagoshima and Kumamoto on business, looking to make a sale.

Ichi's friends were able to furnish information about Teriha. She had taken ill after New Year's and died two weeks later. Rumor had it she'd suffered from lung disease.

"She was from Kurojima," said Shokkichi in a daze. Kurojima was an island about eight and a half miles west of Iojima. "I promised to marry her."

Ichi jumped for joy. "Marry me instead! Make me your wife and take me back to the island. I'm from Iojima like you, not Kurojima." She clung to him through the bars of the lattice.

"But you're just a kid."

Ichi's nostrils flared. "Sleep with me. You'll see I'm a woman all right." She grabbed Shokkichi by the collar and shook him while he stared her in the face. “Do it! Sleep with me!”

She shook him again, and he nodded. “Okay, I’m buying you,” he said, and rushed inside the brothel.

That night, Ichi slept with Shokkichi.

With two pillows on a single futon, they lay stretched out side by side at first, rather like brother and sister. Shokkichi was ill at ease. Not long ago he used to pass her now and then on the beach. She was like a boy then, half-naked. If his eyes happened to meet hers, she’d throw a fistful of sand at him and say, “What’re you lookin’ at?” Here there was no sound of waves. Having Ichi next to him was like a crazy dream.

“Sell any cattle?” Ichi asked. This was the sort of thing people said when he ran into them on the street.

“Yeah, the lot.”

“When’ll you be back?”

“Next spring.”

Ichi contemplated that far-off spring. Since coming here, she’d been unable to think about the future. Tomorrow would bring no more freedom than today. What would her life be like in the spring? She closed her eyes, adrift. Just ahead lay tomorrow. Next year was much further away.

Shokkichi’s body beside her was steeped in the smell of the ocean. It had been washed by the waters of the ocean where she used to swim and play, the ocean stained yellow by the sulfur that gave the island its name. Everything else was veiled in haze; only Shokkichi's body beside her was firmly there, present in the moment.

"Who do you like more, Teriha or me?"

"I just lay down with you, I don't know!"

"I'm healthy, you know. A cowherd's wife has to be. Buy me and take me away."

"You talk too much. Quit yapping!"

He put a hand over her mouth and swung a leg as strong as an oar over her, straddling her. This was why he didn't like prostitutes who were too young. They couldn't take care of you properly and kept making demands.

"If you want me to buy you, be a good horse." He lowered himself onto her and began riding her violently, as if to say his decision rested on the quality of the ride.

"Ow! It hurts. You're hurting me!" Ichi screamed.

"I thought you said you were a woman now!"

"It hurts. Stop. Stop it!"

Ichi burst into tears, and reluctantly Shokkichi peeled himself away. She pressed a hand against her crotch and howled in pain. Worried, Shokkichi put an arm around her small naked shoulders and bent over her.

"You okay? Did something tear?"

He took her hand away from her crotch. Her palm

was dripping with bright red blood. Shokkichi leaped up with a cry of alarm.

Ichi returned to school for the first time in quite a while.

She seemed to be on vacation, showing up not just in the afternoon but all day, every day. Whether she was having her period or not feeling well wasn't clear, but for three or four days in a row she came to the classroom and wrote eagerly.

Girls from the licensed quarter seldom came in the morning, so usually Ichi was the only one there. Tetsuko, too, was busy at that time of day cleaning the school inside and out. By the time she finished and returned to the peach-blossom classroom, Ichi's finished composition would be on her desk. Tetsuko would put on her glasses and pick up the paper.

Ichi kept writing.

Sometimes she would pause to think and take a deep breath, like an ama emerging from the ocean depths, then dive back in. All around her, words swam like a school of fish flicking their tails and fins. Ichi cleaved the water in pursuit, bending and twisting with the suppleness of a mermaid, catching words like fish.

November 29   Aoi Ichi

I have today off.

I can do anything I want.

I thought Id take a bath
or do my laundry
but I didnt do anything.
Like someone who gets candy
and cant bear to eat it
I just lay in bed.
Now thats a real vacation.

December 2 Aoi Ichi
I met a man from home.
He smelled of the sea.
The smell made me homesick
but he was ugly stingy and cowardly
a really nasty man.

Something pattered against the window, and Tetsuko turned her head. Bits of white ice were striking the windowpane. It was hailing.

Tetsuko's heart was torn by emotion as she pictured Ichi making her way back in the cold, pelted by hailstones.

I Sucked White Blood

New Year's came, and for the first time in her life Ichi ate mochi, cakes made from sticky white rice. In Kyushu and the islands scattered in the southern seas, rice was a rare luxury, an imported food. The word "imported" suggests it came from another country, and indeed, to people on islands many miles to the south, Kyushu was as exotic as a foreign land. Growing up, Ichi had never seen a rice paddy, or even rice grains for that matter. Her eyes popped at the sight of the freshly pounded mochi, so stretchy and malleable.

Of the eight hundred or so prostitutes in the quarter, barely half could enjoy the New Year's mochi. But because the Shinonome stood at the apex of all the local brothels, on New Year's morning its eighty prostitutes, including Ichi at the very bottom, were able to eat piping-hot mochi and then, before anyone else, set off for the year's very first bath, taking with them brand-new undergarments courtesy of Mohei.

In the big bath, where green yuzus floated in the hot water, Ichi and Kogin, Kikumaru, Hanaji, and Umekichi washed each other's backs. Like yuzus ripening on the branch, the other girls' breasts and hips had grown rounder and fuller in the past year. Ichi, the youngest and last to take customers, was built like a scrawny monkey in comparison. Even so, now that her initiation was over and she had been promoted to prostitute in training, wearing a bright kimono with flowing sleeves, she had gradually acquired customers who didn't mind someone like her.

Kikumaru and Ichi had each brought a raw egg to the bath. Ichi's was a gift from Shinonome, and Kikumaru's was from the oiran Murasaki, whom she attended. Washing your hair with egg made it as sleek as wakame seaweed. The girls divided the two eggs among the five of them and rubbed the mixture into their wet hair.

"I hope this makes my hair shine," said Ichi as she massaged her hair and scalp.

When they got back, a hairdresser would be waiting for them. At New Year's the girls all dressed in new kimonos, and their hairstyles and makeup were special, too. The entire first week of January consisted of festival days, and the fourteenth and fifteenth were grand festival days, the gayest and most extravagant of all. Every courtesan, high and low, went to great lengths to beautify herself.

On the fourteenth and fifteenth, customers were charged four times the usual rate. On those special days when everything else was on sale, prostitutes' prices doubled and redoubled. Even so, habitual clients made a point of waiting for those costly days to come calling. In the licensed quarter, ordinary society's common sense was stood on its head.

If rates were doubled on festival days and quadrupled on grand festival days, how much must Shinonome's patron pay for the favor of her company? There was also a special fee, payable directly to the oiran, for the privilege of sleeping with her. Her patron was further responsible for gift money in honor of the New Year as well as for her wardrobe and all sorts of other expenses for the coming year.

Some people spent money like water, and others were inundated with the money thus spent. Relations between a man and a woman went smoothly when a good balance was struck. Ichi, however, was still a child and didn't understand such things.

"Looks like Shinonome will have the grand festival days all to herself this month." Kikumaru sighed as she put her arms through the sleeves of her underkimono after her bath.

"Why do you say that? Murasaki will be there, too." Ichi looked puzzled.

Kikumaru lowered her voice. "Oh, then you haven't heard. My oiran's expecting."

"Expecting!" Ichi exclaimed, in a voice so loud that Kikumaru clapped a hand over her mouth.

"Shh!"

"Pregnant? That's serious!" Ichi whispered.

Kikumaru nodded and patted her own belly. "She got careless."

For a prostitute to become pregnant was a blunder of the greatest magnitude. Murasaki's period was irregular anyway, so when she was late she hadn't thought anything of it. A gynecologist came once a month to examine her and Shinonome for signs of venereal disease. Murasaki had a slender build, and she had not been visibly pregnant.

Hajima Mohei swore in a rage he was going to sue the doctor, but it seemed that some women were simply built differently. In the end he did nothing.

If a prostitute became ill, she could be treated and recover, but if she was with child, she would have to take time off until the birth and for a while afterward, while recuperating. The baby would be put in foster care as soon as it was born, but the mother could not return to work until her milk stopped.

"She didn't have any morning sickness ever," said

Kikumaru. "She had a good appetite and put on quite a bit of weight. And then it turned out she was pregnant!"

"Oirans are human, too, after all," said Kogin. "The body is in God's hands, and sometimes there's just nothing you can do about it. It could happen to anybody, getting pregnant like that."

"That's right." Kikumaru nodded. "She was just unlucky." Kikumaru didn't know what the future held for her now. An oiran on leave couldn't provide for her. "She'll stop working as of today."

"Oh, wow," said Ichi.

"She's in her fifth month, and even if she doesn't show much yet, it's just a matter of time."

Everyone sympathized, knowing the same thing could happen to them. Kikumaru had asked around and found that an oiran giving birth wasn't all that unusual. If a lower-tier prostitute became pregnant, she was sent straight to a local obstetrician for either an abortion or an early birth, and the infant's life was lost. But the pregnancy of an oiran, who stood at the apex of hundreds of ordinary brothel girls, was treated differently. A prominent physician was called upon to look after the mother-to-be with utmost care and see that she gave birth safely, without injury to her precious body. If the baby was a girl, she would be put into foster care at great expense, and if she inherited her mother's looks and body, she would be brought back in a few years to undergo training as a candidate for oiran. Baby boys were sold into foster care for next to nothing and never seen again. They had no intrinsic worth. Here, too, the licensed quarter turned society's norms upside down.

Ichi had heard Mohei and his wife, Tose, talking with Shinonome the other day about the *uchikake* over-robe they had ordered this year for her to wear on parade. It was going to be gorgeous, certain to be widely admired and perfect for her solo procession, when all eyes would be on her.

The lavish expense of the uchikake and all other clothes and preparations was of course borne entirely by Shinonome's patron, whom Shinonome induced to pay. That was the power exerted by an oiran.

"It's a big event for her." Kogin sighed.

The Gessho, a rival establishment, had an oiran named Yugiri and would no doubt go all out for her New Year's parade appearance, too. A one-on-one contest would take place between the two oirans on Nakamise Avenue for the whole quarter to see.

Ichi wasn't worried. Shinonome was a natural-born oiran; Yugiri couldn't compete with her. Traversing Nakamise Avenue on high lacquered geta through a throng of onlookers, using the slow, figure-eight gait unique to oirans, Shinonome would wear a bewitching smile. There would not be a trace of anxiety or strain on her face. To Ichi, that was the mark of a true oiran: the total absence of worldly care.

Then what was Shinonome?

Simply the grand queen of female genitalia.

Murasaki, dethroned by her pregnancy, had gone back to being an ordinary woman. The fetus in her womb now reigned over her.

The five of them wound their damp hair on top of their heads and walked back together from the bath in the afternoon. Lit by the New Year's sun, the road shone with unaccustomed beauty.

"On New Year's Day, everything you see or do is a first," said Ichi as they walked along. Tetsuko, their teacher, had taught them this. She pointed to a crow on a rooftop. "That crow up there is the first crow of the New Year." There was a scattering of little birds by the side of the road. "Those are the first sparrows."

Umekichi looked toward the river and grinned. "Over there's the first dog."

"And we're the first girls!" exclaimed Kogin.

Kikumaru, the oldest of the five, began to laugh. "Us? Girls? Hardly! You know what we are? First prostitutes!"

Just then Ichi, who had been walking a bit ahead of the others, let out a cry and came to an abrupt halt.

They had come to the end of a long fence, just around

the corner of which was a back alley they used as a shortcut. As Ichi turned, the toe of her wooden geta touched a pool of red. Her eyes, staring down, turned red, too.

"Wha-what is this!"

It was like water but different, red and thick and viscous.

As Kikumaru, Kogin, Hanaji, and Umekichi came up behind her, they, too, barely stopped themselves from pitching forward. In the red pool a woman lay facedown. Her neck white with makeup, her hairstyle, and her kimono were plainly those of a prostitute. The red liquid had soaked into the kimono, blurring the outlines of her figure, oddly arranged as she lay collapsed on the ground. She looked like a broken doll afloat in a pool of red.

"Ugh." Ichi put a hand over her mouth. She had never seen or smelled such a thing. She felt nauseated.

"M-m-mur . . ." Kogin stuttered.

Murder.

She could not get the word out.

Here it was, a murder in the district. They had heard the older prostitutes talk about affairs that ended in bloodshed, had drawn mental pictures of such scenes. The woman's face was turned down, invisible. There were sharp rips in the back of her kimono and sash. Seeing the red oozing from them, Ichi felt dizzy. She looked away.

They all took a deep breath and shouted, "Murder!" Then they broke into a run.

•

The New Year's holiday ended January 3, but afterward, with the grand festival days just ahead, excitement rebuilt in the quarter. The prostitutes redoubled their efforts amid this atmosphere of gaiety. Anyone who failed to attract customers on those days would lose face both with the house and with her colleagues. Senior prostitutes who seldom attended classes at the Female Industrial School began showing up to practice writing to their patrons.

Hajima Mohei frowned. The New Year's Day murder had gotten the year off to an inauspicious start. Soon, however, everyone was so busy that they forgot all about it. Mohei himself was preoccupied with numbers, trying to calculate how many big-spending clients Shinonome might lure in.

The woman killed in the alley behind the bath had been a prostitute at the Minami. A young fishmonger named Kitagawa murdered her with one of his own sashimi knives, people whispered, inflicting horrible stab wounds to her chest before he jumped into the nearby Kurokawa River—a simpler way to die than turning his knife on himself. Despite Kyushu's temperate climate, the water this year was so icy that he was dead of cardiac arrest before he had time to drown.

The crime cast a pall over New Year's Day, but soon all traces of blood were covered with sand, chilly winds had carried off the floral offerings on the riverbank, and the gossip ceased.

On January 5, the classrooms of the Female Industrial School, each decorated with a pair of large round mochi cakes, were crowded with extra desks for a change. The atmosphere was festive.

In the peach-blossom classroom, older prostitutes who usually stayed away sat alongside the younger girls. Hoping desperately to entice their regular customers to come by on the upcoming grand festival days, they nibbled on the ends of their writing brushes with expressions of fierce concentration.

Tetsuko stood facing the blackboard, her kimono sleeves tied up with a cord as usual. "Do not start out by writing 'Be sure to come' or you will put him off. Any request you make should arise gradually, after the greeting. Let us start with a greeting for the New Year."

> Please accept my sincere wishes for a joyous New Year.

She wrote this out in a firm, beautiful hand, making the chalk clatter against the blackboard.

"Keep it short and simple. If you are not used to writing, this is sufficient. String together too many fancy expressions and he will know that someone helped you."

She surveyed the older students. “Next, thank him for being a regular patron. After that you can make your request.”

> Your devotion, constant as the unchanging green of the pine, makes me very happy, and I thank you from the bottom of my heart.

“Now try mixing in your own words to make what you write more personal.”

She put down her chalk and moved away from the blackboard.

Teaching prostitutes the art of letter writing was tricky. If the models she supplied were too eloquent, the letters would sound false, unless they were written by an oiran or other high-ranking courtesan. A poorly written letter might sound merely ridiculous. It was best to write not with technical skill but from the heart, in a manner the recipient would find charming. But not everybody could find the right tone, neither too heavy nor too light.

Tetsuko went to the desks of the newcomers. Kogin, Hanaji, and the others had laid their brushes down and were talking.

“Ma’am, what should we do?” asked Umekichi. “We don’t have any regular customers.”

“I see. Well, you cannot help that. Copy what is written on the board to practice your calligraphy.”

Tetsuko's eyes traveled to Ichi, who was hunched over her paper, writing. "May I see?"

Ichi looked up and handed her the paper. "I wrote about New Year's Day!"

January 1 Aoi Ichi
This morning we all went to take a bath.
We were the first prostitutes of the New Year.
On the way back we saw the first crow and first
sparrows.
Then we saw a dead woman.
Her back was split open,
blood everywhere.
Her blood was so red.
We shouted and ran away.
The dead body on New Year's Day
was truly pitiful.

Tetsuko had heard of the incident. The dead woman had seldom come to writing class, but she had been avidly learning ikebana and sewing. A merchant had promised to pay off her debt this year and set her up in a house as his mistress. That was why she'd been coming to school. She'd had no interest in the young fishmonger pursuing her.

Bloodshed was common in these parts, but Ichi had never seen such a sight. Since she had grown up on an island, she may have come across a drowned body or two, but Tetsuko believed that of all the ways you could kill a person—hanging, poison, beating—slashing resulted in the most horrific corpse.

After a battle between the forces of the Tokugawa shogunate and those loyal to the emperor at the time of the Meiji Restoration, soldiers' bodies had been piled high around Kan'eiji Temple in Ueno. Her grandfather, who was involved in the cleanup, said that the shogunal troops, felled by bullets, looked fairly decent, but the severely mutilated bodies of imperial troops, slashed by swords, had been a ghastly sight.

Tetsuko closed her eyes and pictured the bloody scene of that long-gone era. Townspeople, men and women who didn't know the first thing about sword fighting, must have found it truly horrifying.

The young girls had stumbled upon the same type of scene, gruesome beyond their imagining, on the first day of the New Year.

Shinonome had never attended the Female Industrial School.

Oirans received special treatment in all things. Shinonome learned calligraphy, poetry, and prose from eminent masters invited to her suite—specialists whose pictures sometimes appeared in the local newspaper. Her suite was also frequented by drapers selling kimonos, masters of go, and heads of ikebana schools. A physician gave her regular checkups, and she was also seen by a gynecologist. Both were well known locally.

The visits of such eminences caused a bit of a flurry, with Hajima Mohei himself serving tea and acting as host. No matter who came to see her, Shinonome remained utterly composed. When the gynecologist came, Tose and other women stayed away, and only Tamagiku and Ichi stayed to assist.

Before the mustachioed doctor in rimless glasses, Shinonome stretched out her legs as smooth as fine white cloth or the firm, translucent flesh of freshly caught squid. Then she opened them wide, raising the curtain on the world, revealing the entrance to paradise.

"One glimpse of that and my cataracts would be cured!" exclaimed the old doorman in charge of footwear.

When the examination was over, a smiling Shinonome saw off the doctor, who strove to give no indication of the pleasure afforded him by what he had seen.

"Murasaki was foolish," said Shinonome, slowly arranging the hem of her kimono. "If she had undergone regular examinations, she would have found out about her condition much sooner. She resisted like a little girl."

After one such session, Shinonome turned to her writing desk. She sat informally with one knee raised, a posture that she liked because it allowed her to air out her crotch. She had little use for a writing instructor because, she said, the written words of a woman of pleasure were empty lies, and masters of writing emphasized sincerity to one's true feelings.

"But I could never be honest with a client I dislike—how could I? Men all come here to enjoy themselves, even the ones who are disagreeable, boring, vulgar, old, or ugly. If a prostitute were always true to her feelings, she would have to tell them she didn't like them and send them all home." She continued to explain while Ichi ground ink. "For a woman of pleasure, lying is a virtue. The lies of an oiran are the greatest virtue of all."

That was why Shinonome had no need for the school's writing instructor, Tetsuko.

"Sincere writing is like the chastity of a woman from the countryside who doesn't know enough to shave her face or put rouge on her lips," she said, laughing.

"Yes'm," murmured Ichi, exchanging glances with Tamagiku.

"It's no favor to the man."

Writing didn't need to be truthful, Shinonome said. She spread out the writing paper and held a narrow brush in her elegant hand. Whatever she did, whether she held a brush or sat with her legs apart, Shinonome was as beautiful as a white moth.

At the beginning of the New Year, I offer you my most joyous wishes for a peaceful year to come.

Shinonome's brush moved swiftly, fluidly across the page. Sentences that didn't come from the heart were easy to write. Ichi peered at the paper, but as the writing was in cursive, which she couldn't read, she had no idea what the letter said. She could tell, however, that the oiran was happy about something.

Then it hit her. Of course! Shinonome wanted this client to pay her a visit and give her a large sum of money during the grand festival days ahead. If she wrote to him, he was sure to come. That was why she was so happy.

> Looking on the unchanging green of the pines, I am reminded of you and your unfailing constancy. It is my cherished wish that you will come to see me during the approaching grand festival days.

Shinonome set aside her brush. "Writing is hard, sincere or not." She put away the rolled letter paper.

Mohei's voice sounded in the hallway. "Oiran, the uchikake is ready. Some people from Daimaru have brought it over. Will you kindly try it on?"

The fusuma slid open and in came two Daimaru clerks, carefully shouldering a voluminous package between them. The robe was heavy, a good fifteen or sixteen pounds, weighed down with plenty of gold brocade and embroidery. Mohei's wife and the two clerks helped

Shinonome into it. With a white dragon and green pines embroidered in gold, silver, and multicolored thread on a background of black silk damask, the robe was dazzling.

Shinonome's heart might be empty and unfeeling, but she was always beautiful. Ichi thought suddenly of Tetsuko at the Female Industrial School, with her dusky skin and prominent forehead. There were all kinds of women.

It was January 14 at last.

Normally the shamisen started up in the evening to signal that the brothels were open for business, but today the playing began briskly in the afternoon. Three musicians would take turns playing until dawn.

Shinonome's favored patron arrived in the afternoon. As the owner of fishing boats and a fishery in Shiranui Bay, he had taken the odd name of Shiranui Taro. His real name was the very ordinary Tanaka Ichisuke, but they were not to call him that. He went by Mr. Shiranui.

This was the man to whom Shinonome had written, *At the beginning of the New Year, I offer you my most joyous wishes.*

He reserved the entire brothel for a private party that night; no other clients were admitted. All eighty Shinonome prostitutes gathered for the event. Ichi, Hanaji, and the other new girls felt relieved, since now they would be employed all evening, filling cups with sake, even though they lacked clients of their own. They were included in the circle of the oiran's radiance.

"What is it about the oiran that makes her patrons willing to spend so much money to be with her?" Ichi asked Tamagiku.

Tamagiku turned her dark, intelligent eyes on the island girl. "That's easy. She has the radiance of Kannon."

"So that's it." With the kamuro, everything was about Kannon.

"You ought to polish the Kannon in you."

The ten-year-old was saucy and precocious.

Upstairs in the grand hall, rows of low tables were laden with food, and geishas with shamisens, drums, and flutes sat in their places, awaiting the arrival of Shiranui Taro. Finally, he and the local merchants he had invited made their entrance, accompanied by the swish of new clothes. The twang of the shamisen and the muffled sound of the drum welcomed them.

Shiranui Taro was a giant. Ichi, however, was not particularly surprised, having grown up accustomed to the men of Satsuma and Iojima. Quite some time after he was seated, the oiran entered, garbed in the splendor of her uchikake robe. She always appeared after her patron, like the star that she was.

Mr. Shiranui welcomed Shinonome as the guest of honor. She sat serenely beside him, and he greeted her with joy. "Oh, Shinonome! Thank you for coming."

The shamisen began to play, and the geishas danced. Ichi sat beside Shinonome and kept an eye on the sake bottle Shinonome and Mr. Shiranui were sharing. Before it became empty, she must signal for a new one to be brought.

"Listen, everyone," Mr. Shiranui announced to the room. "Today I brought breasts of the sea from Shiranui Bay. You can grill them or eat them raw, as you like."

"Breasts of the sea" meant oysters; with the onset of freezing weather, the ban on harvesting them had been lifted. They were called that because they were rich in nutrients. The ones he had brought were enormous, with sharp shells capable of causing an injury when grasped.

"I'll shuck any oyster that goes into Shinonome's mouth," he said. Holding a raw oyster in his left hand and a small knife in his right, he slid the blade in through a slight opening. The shell popped open easily, like the lock on a door. He held a thin towel below Shinonome's mouth and slipped the oyster between her lips. Everyone clapped.

Tamagiku watched with her heart in her mouth, afraid the oiran's uchikake would be soiled.

"I'll open the next one," said Shinonome, but that was impossible. Removing the meat of such an oyster was far beyond the ability of an ordinary woman.

Mr. Shiranui started to protest.

"Kojika, you open it for me."

Mr. Shiranui looked at Ichi in disbelief.

"Yes'm." She picked up the knife and slid it neatly into a shell as big as the palm of her hand.

The patron let out a cry of admiration. "Where are you from?"

"Iojima," she said without further explanation, the word slurred in her southern accent.

"Come again?"

Shinonome explained. "Iojima is an island south of Satsuma. The island where the monk Shunkan was exiled long ago."

"Oh, so you're an island girl. Can you dive like an ama?"

"Yep. But Iojima is so far south that there aren't many oysters."

"What do you catch?"

"Sea bream, horse mackerel, all kinds of fish."

"Go over there and walk for me."

"Sir?" She stood up hesitantly.

"Go on," he said, so she walked along the edge of the tatami while he observed how she carried herself. Her bottom itched from his gaze.

"Good, good." He nodded with satisfaction. "You're a good girl. What's your name?"

"Ichi—I mean Kojika."

"Say, 'My name is Kojika,'" instructed Shinonome.

The banquet ended at midnight. Then Mr. Shiranui would finally be able to take Shinonome to bed, alone.

That was the purpose of the banquet and of his renting the entire place for the night.

When he set off for Shinonome's bedchamber, Mr. Shiranui looked back, holding hands with the oiran, and looked at Ichi with big, bulging eyes. *Remember me*, his eyes said.

He had a face like a big red sea bream.

After the grand festival days, the town fell into a momentary lull. Everyone was tired. There had been widespread approval of the parade down Nakamise Avenue featuring the two oirans, Shinonome and Yugiri. Yet Yugiri was no match for Shinonome; that had been plain for all to see.

Mr. Shiranui sent Shinonome a wardrobe for the entire year. Tamagiku and Ichi also received a large quantity of kimonos. Ichi briefly recalled the face of the man with sea bream eyes.

Without visits from her friend Murasaki, Shinonome seemed lonely. The two of them used to pluck each other's pubic hair, almost as if performing cunnilingus on each other. Now Shinonome's Tamagiku took over the task.

When Ichi had time during the day, she took to dropping by Murasaki's room. Time passed at a leisurely pace there. Murasaki read books and napped. She seemed to be getting enough rest for a lifetime.

But she was an oiran after all, and even during this

extended break she indulged in luxury, making light green tea and sipping it.

"The world is too busy," she said, her red lips breaking into an easy smile.

Most expectant mothers sewed diapers and baby clothes, but since the child would be put into foster care as soon as it was born, Murasaki didn't do anything maternal. She seemed to be at loose ends. Although she was keeping up her beauty routines, her white, waxen complexion was covered in slight blemishes. She wasn't pretty anymore, which made Ichi sad. Her skin was sallow and puffy, the skin of a pregnant woman. To Ichi, Murasaki looked dreary, as if the blood circulating inside her had grown viscous and stagnant.

"When'll the baby be born?"

"Early summer."

Until then Murasaki would go on sharing her body with the child, however uncomfortable that might be. The two of them were one. When you thought about pregnancy that way, it made sense that there was no room for a man.

"I'm just entering my fifth month. The funny thing is, my breasts have already started to produce milk."

"Really? Even though the baby's not here yet?"

Murasaki nodded and pulled the front of her kimono open to reveal her blue-veined chest and her naked breasts. Neither too big nor too small, the breasts of an oiran were elegant. In a man's hands they felt as full and heavy as a pair of ripe, rich peaches. Now blue veins ran across her soft skin, making her breasts resemble white peaches starting to go bad.

She gently pressed one breast, and a bead of white milk formed. It was a murky white, very unappealing. Ichi made a face.

"Want to taste it?" said Murasaki.

Ichi hesitated, but before she quite knew what she was doing she had stuck out her tongue and craned her neck toward Murasaki's nipple. She wrapped her tongue around the white drop.

Murasaki let out a low sigh, her eyes closed.

"Ew." Ichi grimaced. The liquid had an unpleasant smell and taste.

"What's it like?"

"Kind of salty."

There was indeed a faint saltiness mixed in. It reminded Ichi of the time she had cut her finger and tasted her own blood.

The Female Industrial School was quiet again. Five or six new girls had joined the peach-blossom class, but the senior prostitutes were gone, and the classroom was peaceful.

Tetsuko had the girls write about their day as usual, and after they left she picked up their papers with anticipation. Slowly she put on her glasses and began to read.

January 17 Aoi Ichi
The oiran Murasaki is starting to show.
She wont give birth till June but
already shes producing a little milk.
Drink it she said.
I stuck out my tongue and sucked on her breast.
It was a smelly liquid like white smoke.
Drink some more she said
so I stuck out my tongue and
sucked smelly milk again.
Feels like in the New Year
I drank human blood.

Tetsuko removed her glasses and wondered: When this girl grew into a full-fledged prostitute, what sort of love letters would she write?

We Merged

Day by day the peach blossoms swelled, filling Ichi's heart with excitement. As the thin band on each bud loosened and fell away like a woman's kimono sash, here and there on the branches pink-tinged petals opened wide.

Whenever she looked out the window at this sight, Ichi thought of Murasaki, who with her delivery date drawing near had gone off to Nezu village to have her baby in a villa owned by the brothel. As the weather grew warmer and her waist expanded, the mere sight of a stiff kimono sash embroidered with threads of silver and gold had made Murasaki uncomfortable. Now, off in Nezu, she could remove her sash and let her belly grow without worrying about what anyone might think.

Yesterday a letter from Murasaki had come for Shinonome. Even though Murasaki had this extended time off from work, her condition prevented her from going to the theater or other entertainments, so perhaps she felt an urge to write. Shinonome showed Ichi the letter, but Ichi could not read the beautifully flowing, curved black lines.

> On this quiet day in the season of the Doll Festival, I take up my brush to write to you. The constant loneliness and tedium of my Nezu hideaway is impossible to bear. I yearn for companionship. The days are growing longer. Could you come visit me during your time of red silk? I await your answer.

"Red silk" was how the courtesans referred to their periods. Not even the spoiled oirans, so used to having the best of everything and always getting their way, could take time off work for any reason except illness or red silk. Murasaki was asking Shinonome to visit her when the latter opportunity arose.

"I want to go, too." Ichi leaned forward eagerly.

Shinonome shrugged. "I'll be going on *my* red silk days. There's no guarantee you'll be able to come, too."

"Red silk is catching. It'll work out." Ichi smiled and nodded. "I'll stick close by you, so I'll be sure to catch it. Wait and see."

Shinonome couldn't help laughing. While women living together often did start their periods on the same day, it was far from certain that menstruation was contagious.

"When does your red silk start?" asked Ichi.

"Toward the end of the month this month."

"Oh, I can't wait!" Ichi cried out, as if looking forward to some marvelous adventure.

Red silk meant that for a stretch of six or seven days, a prostitute was unable to take clients. The prostitutes had virtually no other time off work. They took clients daily, but sometimes there were no clients to be had, so they were grateful for the chance to earn money when they could.

Ichi worked, too. Little by little, her body adjusted to the routine.

Every day, in a room spread with futons on the fourth floor, the *yarite* Otoku taught them how to handle a client. A yarite was a former prostitute who had grown too old to work and instead took over the education of young prostitutes. Reading, writing, and sewing were taught at the Female Industrial School; sexual skills they learned under Otoku's tutelage.

"You mustn't listen to everything the client says. He wants to do it with you as many times as he can. He wants to get the most for his money and do it on and on without end. If you let him, you'll end up getting injured. You'll get sick and shorten your life. Then what should a girl do to give herself a rest and pleasure the customer? Kojika?" The tip of the bamboo sewing ruler in Otoku's hand touched Ichi on the chest.

"Yes'm. She should pleasure him using prostitutes' special techniques!"

"Come show us." Otoku's ruler tapped the thin futon spread in front of the girls. Then she called to the young man sitting hunched in a corner, whom she had summoned earlier: "You be the customer, Hisakichi. Come on over here and lie down."

Hisakichi stood up, looking pale, and lay down on the futon face up, as instructed. Here in the licensed quarter, male workers had to perform tasks unlike anything they might be asked to do in the outside world.

As the assembled girls stared at him, Hisakichi's face went from pale to bright red. Ichi, equally flustered, joined him on the futon. She started to lie down beside him, but Otoku's ruler hit her smartly on the rump.

"Idiot! What kind of prostitute lies down next to her customer? Show us those 'special techniques.' Show us how to make him come."

Otoku had given a live demonstration the day before, with a servant younger than Hisakichi in the role of customer: seventeen-year-old Takezo, newly arrived from the island of Iki. Poor Takezo had writhed in agony as Otoku, past fifty, set to work with her hands and tongue on his member, which resembled the whitish tip of a bamboo shoot. Alone in bed with a prostitute, no doubt he would have been over the moon, but being held down and forced to participate under a barrage of intense looks from captivated girls had been torture. Otoku's vaunted techniques had only made him suffer, leaving him unable to find release. Only after prolonged exertions had the goal been achieved.

Ichi and her companions fell silent, remembering the previous day's harrowing session. Resigned, Ichi arranged herself on the left as Otoku had demonstrated and began to undo Hisakichi's loincloth. She soon ran into difficulty, for he had a habit of tying the knot tightly. Otoku scolded her. Hisakichi started to undo the loincloth himself and got whacked by the ruler. Perspiring, Ichi finished untying the knot and finally pulled the loincloth away, exposing the young man's nakedness.

Not our lucky day, Ichi thought as she hovered over Hisakichi's crotch, which gave off a strong, grassy smell. A catastrophe for him, poor guy. She murmured an inward apology.

Everyone watched with bated breath, wondering how long the session would last this time, but scarcely had Ichi's fingers clumsily touched him and her tongue come into faint contact with his sex than Hisakichi let out a strangled cry, rolled his eyes, and went limp with exhaustion.

"Pathetic!" said Otoku. "Clients never react with so

little encouragement. Bring in two or three more futons and lay them out here."

The girls hurriedly did so.

"Now go downstairs and find two or three more men."

Several of the girls went downstairs in search of male workers. Soon three unfortunates were led into the room.

"Good, good. You men lie down. Kikumaru, Ayano, and Yumikichi, you come join them."

Three couples stretched out on three sets of intensely red bedding. One, two, three living hells. Next stop, paradise.

Standing firmly with her feet apart, Otoku gave the signal: "Begin!"

"Don't be so annoying! Why do you stay so close to me? Shoo!" Shinonome brushed Ichi off as if she were a puppy.

"Yes'm." Ichi sprang away, but she was soon right back beside the oiran. "Have you got *he*? I'll give you a massage." She gestured with both hands.

Back home, "he" could refer to volcanic ash; a fly, the insect that lands on food; a fart; and also, for some reason, stiff shoulders. People from elsewhere wondered how a monosyllable could express both "stiff" and "shoulders," but in any case, that was the word islanders used.

Shinonome, of course, didn't know any of this. She

scowled and berated Ichi for using coarse language: Only men said "he." Women in the licensed quarter always used the politer word *onara* for "fart." But even that applied only to ordinary prostitutes. For oirans, the word "onara" did not exist. She herself had never done such a thing, Shinonome concluded, completely missing Ichi's point.

No, no. I just want to be near you. Ichi began to massage Shinonome's shoulders. Even back on the island, she had always been good at giving massages.

Shinonome fell silent, enjoying the sensation.

Lately, whenever Ichi wasn't working, she clung like a burr to Shinonome's side. She wanted to "catch" the oiran's period so that they could have time off together and go visit Murasaki.

Was other people's red silk really so contagious? Shinonome wondered to herself, her eyes closed. "Contagious" made it sound like some dreadful disease. Disease was to be shunned, but a woman's period was part of the normal workings of her body. How could that life process spread from woman to woman? It seemed as if the body were controlled by some nebulous living substance resembling invisible gas or smoke.

When Shinonome was a child, her grandmother had taken her to a clinic for acupuncture and moxibustion, where she'd looked at an old-fashioned book bound with thread. The cover bore the title *Acupuncture*

Notes. Inside were color drawings of bizarre worms and other creatures. Worms inhabiting the stomach, called *chishaku*, were red with horizontal stripes and finlike appendages. They caused trouble.

Kammushi were white with a blue back. They had arms but no legs, only something like a long tail. When those worms got into the liver, you developed a taste for spicy foods. "Your father has kammushi," Shinonome's grandmother used to say.

Her grandmother also told her about *kagemushi*, which wreaked havoc in a woman's body. When they took hold, she said, the woman became "debauched"—a word Shinonome hadn't understood—and her uterus filled with blood. What could it mean to have the uterus fill with blood? Her grandmother and the old woman who practiced acupuncture and moxibustion were both long gone, so she couldn't ask them. Maybe that worm was responsible for menstruation.

With her eyes closed, Shinonome let her thoughts continue to drift.

The illustration of a kagemushi had resembled a long, fat, white earthworm covered with beautiful red horizontal stripes. Ichi's fingers stroked on and on, pressing deep into her muscles. Something seemed to seep from Ichi's fingertips into Shinonome's body.

How was a woman's body made, anyway? Shinonome imagined menstruation worms. Sometimes prostitutes sharing a room did mysteriously have their periods at the same time. Close friends would sometimes start bleeding together. Then Otoku would conduct inspections to make sure no one was faking to get out of work.

Would she and this monkey-like girl really get their periods at the same time? Shinonome had the queer sensation that Ichi's fingers were probing deep inside her body.

One afternoon at school, Ichi was sitting as usual at the desk by the window, hunched over and writing assiduously in her notebook.

March 18 Aoi Ichi
On my next vacation Im going to visit
Murasaki.
Shes lonesome so she wants visitors to come
soon.
The oiran Shinonome promised I can go too.
The kamuro Tamagiku wants to go with us but
she cant.
Shes still too young to have her period.
Girls who have no period have no red silk days.
If you have no days off you cant go.
Tamagiku is still a child.

Tetsuko came over by Ichi and read what she had written. The sentences were full of happiness.

"When are your red silk days?" she asked.

Ichi smiled broadly. "Don't know yet. It's like asking when a bird'll fly. You don't know till it happens."

What a funny girl she was, thought Tetsuko. If the day her period would begin was as unpredictable as the moment a bird took flight, how could she be so sure of coinciding with Shinonome?

"It's easy. My mother and the other amas on the island always used to take their time off together."

"How did they manage that?"

Kogin, Kikumaru, and the others pricked up their ears when they heard Tetsuko ask this. Ichi occasionally made mysterious declarations.

"Among close friends, periods are catching. That's what they told me."

Everyone exchanged surprised looks.

"That is all there is to it?"

Ichi nodded.

Her mother and the other women stayed naked most of the time, except in winter. They all had sleek bodies of burnished bronze, and they did everything together. Friends would gather on the rocks or on the shore around a bonfire to dig for clams, sharpen knives, or comb each other's hair, chatting. That was all it took. Several of them would begin their periods together and take time off as if by prearrangement.

"They merged," she said.

The class tittered.

Ichi clearly was convinced of what she was saying, so Tetsuko and Ichi's companions said nothing.

"Oh, I can't wait!" Ichi looked out the window. Soon now she would be able to leave the licensed quarter. She was looking forward to seeing Murasaki again, but she was thrilled to be going outside.

Turning back to her inkstone, Ichi ground some more ink. Then she picked up her brush and wrote again in characters resembling sea slugs:

> This is a peculiar place.
> Outside there are houses and streets but beyond
> that theres another bigger outside.
> I realized it after Murasaki went to live in Nezu.
> She went outside the outside to have her baby.
> What does this place look like from outside the
> outside?
> Are there big roofs?
> High above this sky are there roofs still bigger,
> higher?
> I want to see all the peculiar sights.

Shinonome had just started to undress in the bath in the Shinonome when she spotted something running like a thread down the inside of her right leg. She opened her silk underskirt and saw a trail of blood that went from her thigh to her ankle. She took off her underkimono, carefully washed the skirt, and immersed herself in bathwater illuminated by the morning sunshine.

No wonder she had been feeling slightly swollen since yesterday, as if impure fluids were stagnating inside her, dulling her skin, making her puffy, and causing an occasional twinge of pain in her lower abdomen. After washing herself she returned to her room and sent Tamagiku down to the office with a message: "Tell them that the oiran is beginning her red silk leave."

She was not surprised when a shadow fell on the shoji door and Ichi poked her head around the corner, smiling with irrepressible glee.

"You too?"

"Yep!" Eyes shining, Ichi nodded.

"When did you start?"

"Yesterday morning."

So Ichi had been first. Shinonome looked a bit put out. She wasn't pleased to feel this young girl influencing her.

That afternoon, Shinonome wrote a letter.

> In regard to your recent invitation, this month the red silk visitor has come a bit early, so I plan to call on you in four or five days. I hope you are well. If any day is inconvenient for you, please let me know. The monkey child from the island

wants to accompany me, so I will bring her along and have her carry some fragrant sprays of peach blossom for you.

She asked at the office that the letter be given to the porter.

For the next three days, Shinonome rested comfortably in her suite. She would go out on the fourth and fifth days, when the flow had lessened. Ichi, looking bored, played catch with Tamagiku using beanbags.

With two women menstruating in a closed room all day, there was a faint smell of blood in the air. Or rather than blood, the smell of rusty metal, Shinonome thought. It struck her as vaguely ominous. She was annoyed, even though the smell was partly hers. Not even impoverished prostitutes unable to afford a rest could carry on their trade during their time of the month, and this was the reason. Being a woman was impractical, Shinonome concluded, sitting by the hibachi with one knee raised and holding her long thin pipe in one hand as she blew out a stream of smoke.

The fourth day was unfortunately rainy, but the fifth was a day of tranquil spring sunshine, just right for the trip to Nezu that Ichi had been so eagerly awaiting. Her heart danced as she put her arms through the sleeves of her best kimono. Outside, a rickshaw arrived.

Shinonome stepped out carrying a parasol and wearing a kimono of pale purple figured satin with a sash of thick silk scattered with cherry blossoms. Ichi, seeing Shinonome outdoors for the first time, thought her as dazzling as a ray of sunlight.

How beautiful, she thought, overwhelmed. Under a light coat of makeup, Shinonome's skin had the white translucency of a silkworm. She seemed to emit the radiance of paradise.

The rickshaw set off, followed on foot by two men with strong arms and Ichi, carrying an armful of peach-blossom sprays. The men were Shinonome's bodyguards. There was no telling who might be lurking in the outside world: men who had given the oiran up after running out of funds; men who had bankrupted themselves for her; men who, unable to afford her in the first place, could only stare at her in the oiran procession with resentful longing.

Shinonome was a living strongbox. Ichi had never seen such a thing, but she had heard that in the outside world, fancy brick theaters and trading companies had safes that held piles of money. Shinonome's stepping out into town was like a strongbox going out and about, Ichi thought. A menstruating strongbox! She laughed to herself.

She followed the rickshaw through the large gate marking the entrance to the pleasure quarter. Last year when she passed this way, she'd come from Shimabara Bay, the harbor where her boat had docked. She couldn't remember the route they had taken from there. Beyond the gate was the wide Shirakawa River; they crossed a long bridge to the other side, toward human habitation.

The river's current looked fast. There were guardhouses on either end of the bridge, so a woman seeking to escape would have to jump into the river. Only someone raised on an island would have the necessary strength to swim to the other side.

On the other side of the river, the road passed through fields of daikon. The pleasure quarter was kept separate from town. Between a prostitute's legs lay hell, people said and drew a firm line between the human realm and a place with so many hells. That was the reason for the interminable fields of daikon.

Once past the fields, they came upon houses, then the town. Merchant houses lined a broad avenue on either side, followed by a scattering of fine brick buildings in the Western style.

Beyond the avenue were the stone parapets and high turrets of a great castle. White walls and splendid roofs of black tile stood out amid the surrounding greenery. The castle tower and many of the turrets had been destroyed by fire in the Satsuma Rebellion of 1878, and some of the walls had collapsed. The Shinonome was imposing, too, but it was no match for the castle. The town must be many times bigger than Iojima.

All the clients who purchased Shinonome and Ichi came this way. *The oiran and I certainly live in a tiny place.*

The sky above the castle town stretched overhead like an enormous white parasol. The town seemed as immense to Ichi as the ocean around her island. Nezu was on the far edge of town, by a bamboo grove. By the time they arrived, they'd been walking the better part of an hour, Ichi thought. The villa had a gate, a big garden, lots of tatami rooms, and a teahouse.

Murasaki came out to greet them.

After ushering the rickshaw driver and bodyguards into a small room where they could relax, Murasaki led Shinonome and Ichi to her room. She was shaped like a long-necked sake bottle, with a prominent round belly. Her neck and shoulders were pitifully thin. She was due to give birth in June, she said, less than three months away.

"My face is such a mess, I'm ashamed."

Light brown blemishes covered her face, drowning her eyebrows, eyes, and mouth.

"Not at all. You look lovely." Shinonome's voice was stiff.

Out of habit, the two women addressed each other in the language peculiar to the licensed quarter, but with her loose hair and ordinary kimono sash, Murasaki looked nothing like an oiran.

Half-sewn baby clothes lay on a cushion by the writing desk. Since the infant would be going straight into a foster home, Murasaki had previously said she wouldn't be doing any sewing, that her body was a mere conduit. What had changed?

"I thought supplying the foster mother with a few baby outfits might help," she said hesitantly.

"Yes, of course. A great help, no doubt," Shinonome was quick to agree.

"I want to touch your belly," said Ichi.

Murasaki slowly unwound her wide sash and presented her belly to Ichi. When Ichi laid her hand on the kimono covering it, she felt something move. She cried out in surprise and pulled away.

"It moves a lot. Look, here's a foot."

She guided Ichi's hand. Yes, something was definitely protruding. Probably a heel, Murasaki said. The baby kicked its heels against her belly, sometimes with amazing force, she said.

Something hard, an arm or a leg, abruptly changed position beneath Ichi's hand.

"It's mad about something. When it gets mad, it kicks." Murasaki wiped her eyes with the corner of her kimono sleeve.

Ichi and Shinonome exchanged glances. The baby that was supposed to be merely passing through had begun to capture Murasaki's heart.

Murasaki's body smelled faintly of milk. Shinonome recalled the dark interior of the storehouse at her maternal grandparents' place in the countryside. The dark space was filled with large tubs of soy sauce and miso that gradually matured over a period of six months. Murasaki's body was like a tub where slender bones came into being, limbs took shape, an infant's body formed, and milk accumulated. The more what was inside her grew, the greater her suffering.

At noon, special bento boxes for peach-blossom viewing were delivered. They ate together, facing the garden, where plum and peach blossoms were at their peak. Ichi thought it was like the Doll Festival.

The afternoon shadows lengthened, and sometime after three o'clock Shinonome prepared tea. Once they had finished their tea, they said goodbye.

On the way back through the bamboo grove, Shinonome walked with Ichi ahead of the rickshaw and the bodyguards.

"I might end up alone." Shinonome kicked a pebble. "I might lose a good friend."

Women sold into prostitution were separated from their parents and siblings. As alone in the world as if they had been disowned, they lost all blood relations. Their colleagues became a second family to them, companions in their life of suffering. Shinonome was lonesome.

Ichi, too, suspected that Murasaki might not come back after she had the baby. Unlike prostitutes with no resources, as an oiran she could leave the pleasure quarter and live with her child if she so chose.

Shinonome kicked another small stone. "A woman's body is a funny thing," she said. "Having a child inside touches a woman's heart."

Ichi remembered touching Murasaki's breast. Maybe Murasaki had gotten pregnant on purpose because she wanted a child.

As they came out of the bamboo grove and into town, Shinonome climbed into the rickshaw. Soon they were back on the broad avenue lined with merchant houses. As the high castle tower came into view, Shinonome turned and looked back. Ichi's footsteps were dragging, and she lagged behind.

Ichi pointed wordlessly to her feet. Shinonome's eyes opened wide. Beneath her kimono hem, Ichi's feet were covered in blood. In the course of the long walk, blood had dripped down her legs. Fortunately the bodyguards hadn't noticed.

The street had gradually become livelier, more crowded. If Shinonome kept looking back, the men would notice. She faced forward again, her heart racing.

"I feel a little sick to my stomach," she said. "Please slow down." The driver obediently slowed his pace.

Ichi was young and healthy, capable of a strong

blood flow, so even on her sixth day they should have been more careful. Shinonome regretted not having looked out for her more. She felt as if her own feet were getting wet along with Ichi's.

Now and then their eyes met, exchanging unspoken messages:

Are you okay?

I'm okay.

After they had passed through the part of town with rows of fancy Western-style buildings, they came to a residential area with houses that had low roofs. Shinonome had the rickshaw stop in front of a small candy store with sagging eaves. Beside the store entrance was a small, shabby doorway with a nameplate reading "Akae." Illiterate prostitutes sometimes showed up here asking for something to be written out. A former prostitute living upstairs did the job for them.

Shinonome pretended to be sick from riding in the rickshaw and had the driver and bodyguards wait while she took Ichi up to the house. When she called out, a woman wearing no makeup came to the door.

"Might I ask a small favor?" Shinonome pushed Ichi inside the entryway. They were led upstairs to a woman's small, plain room.

"Teacher!" Ichi flew over to Tetsuko.

"Goodness, what happened?"

Shinonome explained, and Tetsuko quickly peeled

off Ichi's tabi socks. Then she fetched water from the well below, washed Ichi clean, and brought her a change of underclothes.

"I see. So today was your red silk holiday, is that it?"

Ichi sat down to put on a borrowed pair of tabi. "Not only me. The oiran, too. We merged." Ichi looked at Shinonome, standing by the window in the dim room like a rainbow.

Shinonome's and Tetsuko's eyes met for the first time. Shinonome smiled, so Tetsuko did too. They both still felt awkward, but gradually the tension eased.

The red silk holiday was over.

Sunshine flooded the streets of the small pleasure quarter. Ichi was eager to be active again, and the first thing she wanted to do was go to school. As she was about to rush off in the morning with her slate, paper, and inkstone, Shinonome called to her and thrust a piece of paper in her hand—a letter, evidently.

"Give this to your teacher with my best regards," Shinonome said softly.

When Ichi arrived at the Female Industrial School, she went straight to Tetsuko's desk. After thanking Tetsuko for her help, she handed her the letter from Shinonome. Then she went to her seat and began grinding ink. The smell of ink soothed her spirit.

Tetsuko put on her glasses and opened the letter,

a brief message written in a distinctive feminine hand. The lines looked like an arrangement of beautiful vines.

> The other day we caused you considerable bother. Despite our sudden arrival, you generously came to the rescue, and Kojika and I were both relieved. Please accept my most humble gratitude. Also, please continue to teach Kojika to write.
>
> One in my position becomes so steeped in the courtesan mentality that writing from the heart is impossible. No expressions of genuine feeling come to mind. I merely arrange empty words on the page as my trade demands and amuse myself by composing clumsy verses like this one.
>
> *Pleasure of a courtesan—*
> *on Doll's Day*
> *smoking a pipe*
>
> Hoping that this may make you smile,
>
> Shinonome

Tetsuko looked at the letter for a while before folding it and tucking it into the breast of her kimono as if to warm it. As Ichi was leaving, Tetsuko handed her a similar letter to give to Shinonome.

By evening, the letter was in Shinonome's hands. Once again, she sat with one knee raised, letting out a stream of smoke from her long thin pipe. She opened the letter and found the briefest of messages:

I appreciated your letter.
In return, I, too, have composed a verse.

On Peach Day
I severed all ties
with family

Tetsuko

I Was a Scabbardfish

"What are you doing?" Tamagiku asked, lying in bed with her eyes half-open.

"Nothing a child would understand." Ichi was standing in a corner of the room in her nightclothes. It was late at night.

"Well, I can't sleep with you standing there like a ghost. It's spooky."

Sometimes a new prostitute who had jumped in the river and drowned would return to her room late at night, clinging to the wall like a big nocturnal spider.

"Sorry, sorry. I'm almost done."

Tamagiku pulled the covers over her head, resigned.

Lately, on nights when she had no clients, Ichi had a peculiar bedtime ritual. She would stand next to the wall and, holding herself perfectly still and perfectly erect, breathe deeply in and out.

Shinonome wasn't there. She was off working. An important client had arrived that evening, and after the banquet Tamagiku and Ichi had retired to this back room to sleep. Meanwhile, Shinonome, magnificent in tortoiseshell hairpins and an alluring raiment, was a grand ship just setting out on the night sea with her client aboard.

Ichi's eyes were shut.

Shinonome's voice sounded in her ear: *I can't believe it. You're telling me that a girl of nearly seventeen doesn't know how to stop the flow of menstrual blood?*

Shinonome had said this just the other day, in reference to Ichi's unfortunate mishap on the way back from their visit with Murasaki. Fortunately, neither the rickshaw driver nor the bodyguards had noticed. When Shinonome and Ichi ran inside the home of Akae Tetsuko, Ichi's teacher, and got help in the nick of time, Ichi had been embarrassed, and no doubt Shinonome had been, too.

"Your mother on the island never taught you what to do?"

When Shinonome told her she was supposed to control the flow of blood, Ichi had been amazed in turn.

"Then on the island where you were born, your mother, your sister, and everybody else just walks around letting blood run down their legs?"

Ichi shook her head. No, they didn't do that. Her mother and sister and the other grown-up women used to lie half-naked on the beach, their glistening bodies exposed to the sun. When their periods started, they came out of the water, of course, but Ichi had never seen their clothing stained with blood. So how had they managed?

Shinonome said that a woman having her period was supposed to stop the flow by clenching her vagina and then releasing the accumulated blood every so often into the toilet. This was basic feminine hygiene, she said.

Ichi had had her first period just before being sold here, so there hadn't been time for her mother to tell her such a thing. They had waited for her to begin menstruating and then sold her off immediately.

Seeing Ichi hang her head, Shinonome seemed to take pity on her. "Well, it's all right. Your body is toned from swimming in the sea, and you're as sensitive as a fish. You'll learn in no time."

Then Shinonome told Ichi to stand in front of her. "Ready? Close your eyes."

Ichi did so.

Shinonome spoke softly and gently. "Imagine a straw. Try to picture it."

A piece of straw took dim shape in Ichi's mind.

"Can you see it?"

"Yes'm."

"Now take that straw and hold it in your mouth below."

"My what?"

"You know, the one between your legs. Under your skirt."

Ah. Ichi understood.

Down below, far away, Ichi's vagina began to tremble. Strangely enough, when she focused her mind on that part of her body, it grew warm, as if a tiny lantern had been lit. In her mind she moved the straw slowly toward the mouth under her skirt, then carefully inserted it.

She was doing all this mentally, so she didn't know how much to clench the mouth under her skirt. If she didn't grip the straw tightly enough, it would fall out. She tightened her grip, then tightened it some more.

"Did you do it?"

Still standing, Ichi nodded. Normally battered and put upon, subjected to constant abuse, the mouth under her skirt was now confusingly tasked with holding a slender, lightweight straw.

"Once you are holding the straw, count to ten. Then blow it out."

One, two, three . . . She counted to ten and then tried to expel the straw as if by spitting. It didn't work. "Go ahead," Shinonome encouraged her, but the straw stayed in place, dangling.

Ichi tried over and over. Finally, after many attempts, the straw flew out. "Aha!" Ichi laughed.

"You did it, didn't you?" Shinonome smiled. "Now

start over from the beginning. Imagine a straw. Bring it down there and hold it in the mouth under your skirt. Count to ten and blow it out. One, two, three, four . . ."

At first Ichi managed awkwardly, but as she practiced night after night, gradually the mouth under her skirt began to expand and contract with ease, just like the lips of her other mouth that could eat and talk.

Shinonome said not to forget that sensation. Next month when Ichi's red silk came, she would see the fruit of her efforts. "This is really to help you with your work."

Tamagiku was by now sound asleep, breathing peacefully. When Ichi had dispatched ten straws, she crawled onto the futon laid out next to Tamagiku's and quickly fell asleep.

The cherry blossoms on the trees lining the street scattered, and new green leaves appeared. In early April, the road to the bathhouse was flooded with dazzling sunshine. The Shirakawa River shone as if strewn with fish scales of sparkling silver.

Kogin was walking alongside Hanaji. "Have you ever seen a big ship?" she asked.

Hanaji was from a mountain village in Miyazaki. "No, cows were the only moving thing I ever saw."

"Ships are beautiful," said Kogin. "The way they glide across the water, they're like the most beautiful sea creatures ever." Then she shared news she had overheard in the office. “Guess what? Workers at the shipyard foundry have gone on strike.”

“Strike?”

None of the others had ever heard the word.

“It means workers all get together and stop work. A lot of the foundry workers have gone on strike to protest working conditions at the shipyard.”

“Wow! Then they can’t make any ships.” The factory must be in real trouble, Ichi thought. There would be an uproar if all the workers quit at once.

“Right,” said Kogin. “The shipyard and the ship-owners are in a bind. So apparently they’re improving conditions for the workers.”

Bargaining for improved working conditions was unheard of. The newspapers had devoted considerable coverage to the row.

“Bosses are powerful and employees are weak,” said Kogin. “This time the employees all got together and turned things upside down.” She looked as triumphant as if she were personally involved.

“Wow!” Kikumaru exclaimed. “Going on strike is a great thing!”

“Yeah, but what if the bath attendants at the Asahi-yu went on strike? There are only three of them, so they’d get the heave-ho. Management would be only too happy to wash their hands of them.” Kogin, the eldest of the group, said this with cool, matter-of-fact, big-sisterly wisdom, and everyone laughed.

Ichi thought of the fishermen back on her island. They and the divers, male and female, together made nearly a hundred islanders. Yet none of them had ever gone on strike against their boss. What devoted workers they were, she thought admiringly. Young as she was, she was beginning to understand what it meant to work for someone.

They came to the Asahi-yu and went inside, ducking under the awning and entering the changing area. The morning bath was steamy and empty. This morning, both the women's bath and the men's bath next door were bare and hushed.

First to arrive, Kogin, Kikumaru, Hanaji, Umekichi, and Ichi all undressed and stepped into the bathing area.

Ichi whispered in Umekichi's ear. "Hasn't your period started yet this month?"

"It's over."

"Really? When?"

"Two or three days ago."

And yet Umekichi had come to the bathhouse every day. How?

"Oh, so you want to know about that, do you?" Umekichi laughed easily. "Before coming here, I'd go to the toilet and empty myself all out. After that I could go for nearly an hour without worrying."

So it was true: most girls *did* know how to control the flow of menstrual blood. Imagine that! Ichi wanted to throw back her head and let out a long, hearty laugh. Well, well! The world was a mysterious place, full of things she'd never dreamed of. *All right*, she vowed, *I'll learn to do it, too.*

As Ichi was splashing hot water over herself, Umekichi leaned near. "Kojika, if I ever called for us to go on strike, would you do it?" Her eyes were serious.

"Sure. Count me in." Ichi nodded confidently. Anything was possible. She couldn't imagine how Umekichi would organize a strike, but she liked thinking about it.

The two of them sat with their heads close together.

"What kind of strike?" Ichi asked.

"I'd demand all kinds of improvements in our working conditions." Umekichi looked up thoughtfully at the ceiling. Drops of water rolled off her wet cheeks as she began ticking items off on her fingers.

"Number one, lower the price of tobacco. Make it the same as in the tobacco shops in town." The brothels had conspired to raise the price of tobacco in the quarter, to the prostitutes' dismay.

"Number two, provide an allowance for absence from work due to a cold or influenza. If we take clients when we're sick, we risk making them sick, too."

That was sensible, Ichi thought. And when you were sick, you certainly deserved to rest until you felt better.

Kikumaru and Kogin were listening, too. They took turns chiming in.

"Number three, don't charge interest on the clothes we have to buy."

"Number four, stop charging us for charcoal in winter when we don't even have a hibachi."

"Number five, give us fish once every ten days, even if it's dried fish."

Hanaji scoffed. "That won't happen. They'll just say that if we want to eat fish, we should take it from a client's tray."

"What about when we don't have clients?" said Umekichi.

"They'll say a prostitute with no clients doesn't deserve to eat fish."

"Ooh, it makes me so mad! I'm ready to go on strike now!"

As Umekichi's voice rang out, an old man's gravelly voice could be heard from the other side of the wooden partition separating the women's and men's baths: "Not so loud! You never know who might be listening. We can hear every word!"

The five girls fell silent and shrank into themselves.

Just past noon, her face shining after her morning bath, Ichi went to school carrying her inkstone.

In the peach-blossom classroom, Tetsuko was teaching the art of seasonal greetings. "When you write an invitation to a client, you should mention flowers of the season: plum blossom, peach blossom, cherry blossom, or wisteria. Try to write so that we can see the flowers and smell their fragrance."

She smoothly wrote out an example on the blackboard.

> Spring is in the air. Young bush warblers are singing with increasing confidence, and clusters of light purple wisteria grow longer by the day. I hope you are well.

Pointing at the sentence, she said, "Rather than writing simply, 'The wisteria has bloomed,' it has greater impact if you describe how the flower clusters are lengthening. For the bush warblers, instead of writing simply that you hear them singing, suggesting how the chicks are maturing lends depth to the thought."

When she had finished explaining, everyone picked up their brush.

> The days have grown warmer. The long, trailing blooms of wisteria are like the hair ornaments of a girl of fourteen or fifteen.
>
> Tanaka Riu

Tetsuko came around the desks and read what Kogin had written. "Oh, how lovely that wisteria must be! Well done, Tanaka Riu."

Kogin blushed with pleasure.

Tetsuko went over to Ichi's desk by the window. Ichi was writing eagerly, bent over her paper.

"Show me."

"I'm not writing about wisteria." Ichi hastily covered what she had written with her hand. This was most unusual; she normally presented her work without being asked.

"Then what flower are you writing about?"

"No, I'm not showing you!" Ichi pressed herself against the desk.

She was a stubborn thing, so it wouldn't do any good to try to pry her away forcibly. What could she be writing? Tetsuko began to chuckle. "All right. When you have finished your masterpiece, put it on my desk. That gives me something to look forward to!"

Next Hanaji finished writing and handed in her paper. "Read mine, ma'am, will you, please?"

> I went to see the wisteria. The flowers were like an elegant woman, but when I turned my eyes to the base of the tree, I saw it was knobby, wrinkled, and mossy, like the claws

of a monster cat a hundred years old. Beware of beautiful women! From your faithful Hanaji.

Matsuyama Setsu

Tetsuko looked from the words on the page to Hanaji's face, comparing the two. Hanaji had come here an uneducated country girl and now, although outwardly she looked the same, somehow she had learned to write like this.

If these girls sold into prostitution had remained in the countryside, they would have gone their whole lives not knowing how to write, never straining to find words to express the beauty of flowers. They would have led lives where flowers were flowers, birds were birds, trees were trees, and that was that. It was a world without flaws but lacking in subtlety, taste, and suggestion. They would have worn rustic clothes and crawled around in muddy rice paddies, working up a sweat, till they reached the end of their lives as stooped old women. If there was any benefit in becoming a prostitute, it was only the possibility of becoming literate and discovering the power of words.

Standing by Hanaji's desk, Tetsuko was momentarily lost in these thoughts.

Yet there were students of all kinds in this peach-blossom class, some of whom spent the better part of an hour glued to their desks, unable to write a line. But that was fine; they just needed to think of something before the next class. Some of the girls were scheduled to go to the bathhouse in the afternoon, so Tetsuko soon dismissed the class.

The room rang with thank-yous and goodbyes, and then the students' footsteps receded down the hallway.

Tetsuko removed her reading glasses and began to tidy the room. She straightened the desks, swept the floor, and opened the windows to let in fresh air. Then she went to her desk, picked up the paper that Ichi had deposited there moments ago, and began to read with anticipation.

April 8 Aoi Ichi

These days Im training the mouth under my
skirt.
Shinonome said to make it hold a straw.
The mouth under my skirt holds a straw without form.
At first the mouth was surprised
but gradually it became able to move.
One straw
Two straws
Three straws
Four straws
Five straws
Six straws

Seven straws
Eight straws
Nine straws
Ten straws
It feels itchy
Even though the straws have no form the
mouth moves.

Still holding the paper, Tetsuko sank into thought. A number of girls from Satsuma were sold into prostitution here, and for the most part she could understand their dialects, but this essay baffled her.

The "mouth" no doubt referred to the vagina. By "straw" she must mean a thin stalk of grain. As she pictured the two in her mind, the connection dawned on her, and she chuckled.

April 8, continued Aoi Ichi
I asked a colleague
and she said there are lots of ways to do the
training.
Where Hanaji is from they dont use straws.
She says when the mouth above closes tight in
a smile
the mouth below does the same.
Smile
Smile

Smile
Smile
Smile
Smile
Smile
Smile
Smile
Where Hanaji is from
the mouths under the skirts of all the girls are
smiling.

To close the mouth under the skirt while smiling . . . what could it mean? Tetsuko cocked her head, puzzled. Smiling seemed more likely to relax the muscles than tighten them. Perhaps it meant raising the corners of the mouth tightly. Hanaji and other girls where she grew up must have learned a way of smiling suited to the physiques they developed toiling in the rice paddies.

Tetsuko thought back to her own girlhood. Her mother had given her simple advice on how to handle her menstrual flow. During her time of the month, she would wind strips of silk into a ball and stuff it lightly inside herself. That had always sufficed.

Ordinary women, those not of the samurai class, were unfortunate, she thought. They needed a prop like an imaginary straw to train their lower mouths, or they needed to make themselves smile a certain way. Samurai girls brought up before the Restoration had learned to use the halberd and the short sword, so their muscles were taut to begin with.

Tetsuko's halberd instructor had been a woman in her eighties whose body wasn't at all bent or crooked. When she gripped the halberd, she had moved fluidly, controlling the long-range weapon with perfect ease.

A limber body was like a coiled spring. The spring powered the body's muscles. Daughters of samurais had no need of straws or smiles to train their mouths below but achieved the desired result by twirling the halberd and yelling battle cries.

Tetsuko recalled the appearance of the oiran Shinonome, who had entered her home the other day like a ray of sunlight. The oiran's neck and shoulders were slender, but her body, disciplined by dance and even more so by her thorough mastery of the arts of the bedchamber, must be a marvelous spring.

No doubt she needed only to breathe in and her vagina would contract, breathe out and it would relax, while a paroxysm of laughter would surely set off delicate, wavelike reverberations. The lips under her skirt must vibrate when she spoke and twitch in pain when she wept. The body of an oiran, a woman who stood at the pinnacle of all courtesans, must have that sort of sensuality—subtle, exquisite, and refined.

Tetsuko let out a sigh and folded Ichi's paper. From now on, Ichi, too, would acquire such skills.

A week later, as Ichi took her place on display in the evening, she saw a man come walking toward the Shinonome down the still bright street. She recognized him at once as Shokkichi from Iojima. He must have come to sell more cattle. Now, when the waves were gentle, was the ideal time to transport cattle on ships.

"Shokkichi! Hey, Shokkichi!" Ichi rattled the lattice and shouted his name.

Shokkichi, even more sunburned than before, ran up, looking grumpy. "Damn it, don't yell a person's name like that! I might as well be a pumpkin or a potato! How about a little respect?"

"Never mind. Hurry up and come in."

"Is that how you're supposed to greet a customer you haven't seen in a while?"

Irritated by his reproaches, Ichi said, "Oh, be quiet. You're like a fly buzzing around a cow's behind. Did you sell your cattle?"

"Yep."

"Then hurry on in!"

Shokkichi headed for the entrance, fuming.

When he was settled, Ichi brought in sake and food on a small low table.

"Last time, you gave me a scare. You okay today?"

Shokkichi had a worried look as he stirred his bowl of *chazuke*, hot green tea and flavorings over steamed white rice. On his previous visit, Ichi hadn't yet been broken in, and she had ruptured badly. Shokkichi had been really frightened.

"I'm fine. I've been hard at work every night. Nothing could faze me now, not even an arrow or a gun!" Ichi was giddy with high spirits. "I'll show you!"

"Wow, talk about confident!" Shokkichi laughed.

His former favorite, Teriha, the dead prostitute from Kurojima, had been as quiet and unassuming as autumn frost. Ichi, whose personality was either rain or shine, veering from one extreme to the other, was in her own way a comforting presence to a man accustomed to the harshness of island life.

Ichi set the table aside, took Shokkichi by the hand, and led him to the futon. In the beginning she used to wait for the client to draw her into bed, but she never made that mistake now. If you started off by allowing the client to lead you, you played into his hands and became a sex slave lacking all autonomy.

Ichi's short, plump fingers stroked Shokkichi's body, moving gradually inward and then withdrawing again, tantalizing him.

"Damn, you're good . . ." Shokkichi murmured dreamily. "If you're this good, maybe I should marry you."

Ichi had learned a great deal from Shinonome, and

not only how to hold a straw between her legs. Her subsequent training had been in-depth.

"You mustn't think only of tightening your body," Shinonome had cautioned. Relaxing was the main thing. "It's like breathing. When you breathe, first you exhale and then you inhale." You let out a long slow breath, emptying your body of air, and then inhaled deeply. If you did it the other way around, inhaling first, the air already inside you would prevent you from taking much of a breath. It made sense. "It's like that. Your body should always be loose and relaxed. Do you see? Then you tighten it in key places as necessary. Your mouth below, or deeper inside."

Mastering such things made childbirth easy, she said.

"Really? Then Murasaki will have an easy time?"

"Of course she will! Easy in, easy out. No need to worry. Women without the benefit of training like ours must have a tough time of it, both in bed and in childbirth." Shinonome took a hairpin out of her coiffure and scratched her head. "The thing is to hold yourself relaxed and straight. If you go all soft and limp like an octopus or a squid, you'll end up sick."

Shinonome told Ichi to stand up and close her eyes. "You're suspended from on high. There is a cord attached to the top of your head, and you are hanging straight down. The ground is far below you."

Shinonome's voice cast a spell. Instantly, Ichi's body was suspended in a vast, unknown emptiness, a void.

"How does it feel? Your spine feels straight, doesn't it? Remember what that feels like, whether you're sitting, or sleeping, or walking, or crouching. That straight spine is always running through you. Naturally straight and relaxed."

"Hanging in a straight line like that felt good," Ichi told Shokkichi, finishing up the story as she massaged him.

"Like being in the sea," he murmured, his eyes closed.

"The sea?"

"Yeah. Years ago my buddies and I went skin diving off Ikinoshima to catch fish. Way deeper than the amas go."

"I wish I could go somewhere like that." Ichi sighed, resting her cheek on Shokkichi's chest.

"When you dive that deep, the sea is a void. Completely empty. No water even, just your own body, plunging down like an arrow."

"Did your body feel supple?"

"Supple as a fish." He took Ichi in his arms. "You're like a fish, too."

Ichi turned around, mounting Shokkichi. She placed the mouth under her skirt around him and swallowed him. She felt as if she had grown another hand. A hand that could wrap around him, tightening and relaxing its grip at will. There was still some awkwardness, but the difference between now and the first time they slept together was night and day.

Shinonome's voice sounded in her ear. *Murasaki would never make a mistake like that. She wanted to have a baby.*

Would she, Ichi, have Shokkichi's baby? Would he take her away from this land of night, overflowing with sex and debauchery, and let her go home to her island?

Shokkichi stayed with Ichi till morning. As she lay with her head on his shoulder, he told her about the faraway sea she knew nothing of.

He had seen a school of scabbardfish, he said. Scabbardfish were silver, without scales, and longer than Ichi was tall. They swam vertically in deep water, long straight bands of shining silver.

"Perfectly straight, I tell you. Dozens of 'em, straight as can be, floating in the ocean like long swords. What do you reckon they think about, hanging straight up and down in the water like that? It sure looked weird."

When Ichi didn't answer, Shokkichi looked down. She had fallen into a light sleep.

Early one morning, before anyone else had arrived in the peach-blossom classroom, Tetsuko found a piece of paper on her desk. One glimpse of the messy handwriting and she knew who had written it.

April 16   Aoi Ichi

Yesterday I didnt come to school.
Shokkichi from my island came and I had
work.
Then I slept late.
I dreamed I was a scabbardfish
swimming vertically.
Ma and pa and my brothers and sisters
all swam vertically too
perfectly straight.
Ichi welcome home!
said the scabbardfish pa.
From now on lets be together always.
We all swam vertically together.

As the morning sun began to light the streets in the pleasure quarter, Ichi dashed back to the Shinonome.

Celebrating the Baby's Birth

One morning during the hot and sticky rainy season, Ichi slept unusually late. By the time she'd had breakfast and set out for the bathhouse, her friends were long gone. A fine rain was falling out of the bright mid-June sky, shining like grains of sand. The street was silent and deserted. Raindrops lay heavily on the eaves and on the branches of cherry trees lining the street.

As she walked along with the basin containing her bath things tucked under one arm, Ichi told herself that her body felt heavy this morning because it was almost her time of the month. In the mirror her face looked puffy and somber. During red silk days, a woman's body turned damp and humid, like the rainy season.

But there was one good thing about it. The thought banished her yawns. On red silk days, she didn't have to take any clients. Every prostitute got a monthly holiday. Ichi thought of the baby born to Murasaki two weeks ago in Nezu. Tose, the mistress of the brothel, had gone to see the mother and child and reported with delight that the baby was a girl—a future candidate for oiran, just like her mother. The infant's skin was as white as silkworms, and she had a perfect little nose and lips like cherry petals. "I've never seen such a beautiful baby," Tose had declared.

Ichi also wanted to see the baby Murasaki had borne. Murasaki had been just one person, and now there were two. Pregnancy and childbirth were everyday affairs, yet there was definitely something mysterious about it all. A baby didn't just come from nowhere: it was part of the mother's body, and then it wasn't.

Ichi walked on, secluded under her umbrella.

Shinonome had already seen the baby. She had gone with Tose, since her red silk had come a bit early this month. Afterward, she had been pensive.

This happy time for her friend and colleague was not a time of pure rejoicing for Shinonome. She and Murasaki had been extraordinarily close, even tweezing one another's private parts. Together, the two of them had given their all to support this licentious flower garden growing in life's shadows. Now, like the seven colors of the hydrangea, seven emotions brimmed in Shinonome's heart: relief, sympathy, joy, envy, jealousy, loneliness, and desolation.

As Ichi ducked under the awning of Asahi-yu, the

bathhouse, she ran into Hanaji, Kogin, and the rest just coming out, their freshly washed hair still damp. They called out hellos and trooped back.

The steamy changing room was deserted. Ichi undressed and headed to the bathing area, where she could just make out a girl's hazy figure through the steam. The two of them had the place to themselves.

Ichi washed herself carefully, knowing that her period might begin the very next day, and slipped into the hot water for a good soak. The girl washed her hair and got into the tub, too. She had a small but sturdy build; before coming here, she must have worked hard back home helping her parents. She was about the same age as Ichi, but her face already bore the strain of life as a prostitute. Her eyes were timid.

"Um, aren't you Kojika of the Shinonome?" the girl finally asked.

"Yeah, that's me. Who're you?"

"My name's Nazuna. I'm from the Yoshidaya."

Ichi had never heard of the place.

"It's on a backstreet behind Nakamise Avenue."

"Oh."

The Yoshidaya was one of the smallest and least imposing of the brothels in the quarter, so naturally Ichi had never heard the name. Its only selling point was its location within the quarter, on this side of the great gate. Brothels outside the gate were labeled "hells," and there was no telling what horrors took place inside them. The Yoshidaya was at least a member of the association of houses of prostitution.

"I have a little favor to ask." Nazuna's accent was unfamiliar to Ichi. Where could she be from?

"I heard Murasaki of the Shinonome just had a baby. I worked there till two years ago, and she was kind to me. I'd like to go see her and her baby and take her a little present." She spoke haltingly, with the frankness of a country girl.

"You mean you worked at the Shinonome till just before I came?"

"Yeah, till right before."

They both had a thick accent; each understood about half of what the other said. Ichi gathered that they had just missed knowing each other at the Shinonome.

Nazuna had never been to the villa in Nezu. The Yoshidaya was too small to afford a manservant to act as bodyguard, so its prostitutes were unable to set foot outside of the licensed quarter. All prostitutes, even oirans, were forbidden to go out unaccompanied.

"Would you tell the manager of the Shinonome that Nazuna who used to work there wants to go call on the oiran and her baby?"

Ichi could at least do that much. She nodded, but cautioned that she couldn't guarantee Saito would grant permission. He would do as he saw fit.

"That's fine. Thank you!" Nazuna held her palms together and bowed her head in gratitude.

"Where're you from?"

Ichi's ears had grown accustomed to the dialects of Satsuma, Hyuga, and Higo, near the quarter in Kumamoto. Girls from the former provinces of Bungo, Chikuzen, and Chikugo mostly drifted to Yanagimachi, the licensed quarter in Hakata. In between was the Maruyama quarter in Hizen, which trafficked in prostitutes from both north and south Kyushu.

"Chikuzen."

That was far away, up in north Kyushu.

"I was born in the village of Kanezaki, by the water."

So Nazuna was from the northern coast, by the Genkai Sea. She began to wash Ichi's back. Ichi murmured her thanks and closed her eyes. It felt good.

"Is your pa a fisherman?" Ichi asked.

"Yep. He fishes for bonito in Shikoku. Ma's a diver. When she was young, she even dove in Korea."

Next Ichi washed Nazuna's back.

"Any sea turtles where you're from?" Ichi asked. "Really big ones?"

"No, no turtles. But Pa said he saw whales once in Shikoku."

"In Satsuma, whales are called 'parent-fish.'"

"I'd love to see one."

The conversation had gone off on a tangent.

They left the bath and went to get dressed. Ichi was astonished at the shabbiness of Nazuna's underkimono. It was heavily patched and worn thin around the back and hips.

"You used to work at the Shinonome, right? Why sell yourself to the Yoshidaya?"

"Couldn't help it. I'm ugly."

Ichi didn't think so. Nazuna had an ordinary face with small eyes and a flat nose, that's all. If she'd stayed in her village, she'd have gotten married and had children like anybody else.

On the way back, Ichi told Nazuna that her red silk would be starting soon, and she would go to see Murasaki then. "Can you get a day off?"

"Sure." Nazuna nodded.

Could she really, even if she wasn't menstruating? Ichi was doubtful. Normally smaller brothels worked their prostitutes to the bone, night and day.

"It's all right," Nazuna said. "I've worked without time off for quite a while, so they'll say yes. They owe me."

The girls promised to meet at the bath at the same time the next day.

Ichi hurried back and went to see Saito in the office. When she told him about Nazuna, he cocked his head. He didn't recall anyone by that name, but then it was probably a name she'd been assigned at the Yoshidaya.

"I do kind of remember a girl from Kanezaki up in Chikuzen."

He had no objection. "If she wants to tag along with you, fine by me. I'll assign a bodyguard for the day. Hisakichi's tied up, so I'll let you have Takezo instead."

Just like that, permission had been granted. Congratulatory visits to Murasaki and her baby were evidently a special case. The management was anxious for Murasaki to put her baby in foster care and come back quickly, before extended nursing ruined her lovely, jade-like body. They hoped that visits from lively younger women would encourage her to return.

"When you see Murasaki, be sure to tell her you miss her and you want her to come back soon."

"Thank you." For once, Ichi bowed her head politely.

The next morning it rained. When Ichi got to the bathhouse, without bringing any bathing necessities this time, Nazuna was standing there waiting. Ichi went up to her and said in a low voice, "I'm not going in today. Yesterday I felt bloated, and sure enough, today my red silk started."

"Uh-oh!" Nazuna laughed.

"So I'll be going to Nezu earlier than I'd planned. This time tomorrow I'll drop by your place with a bodyguard, so be ready to go."

She went back to the Shinonome with a bounce in her step.

The next morning, luckily the rain had stopped and the sun was out.

Seventeen-year-old Takezo, their bodyguard for the day, emerged from the brothel carrying a gift package of fruit. Shinonome handed Ichi some Uji tea to take with her as a gift. When Shinonome went anywhere, a rickshaw came for her, but Ichi of course traveled by foot wherever she went.

"We're leaving!" Ichi called.

Old Otoku came outside to see them off. "Takezo," she said, "you'll be responsible for two women, so keep your wits about you."

Ichi and Takezo set off at a quick pace down Nakamise Avenue, Ichi in the lead. Takezo's stride was so long that he kept coming up almost beside her. Then she would shoo him away like a dog: "Get back! Don't come so close."

Takezo clucked in exasperation. The other day Otoku had conducted another training session, and Ichi had been avoiding him ever since. In that third-floor chamber of hell, Ichi and he had performed in front of everyone, playing the parts of a prostitute and her client. For Takezo, it was the second time in his life he had been with a woman. A young servant like him with no money was rarely given the chance to have sex. Now every time he saw Ichi, he was like a hungry dog hanging around in hope of food. His first experience had been with old Otoku.

But Takezo could barely remember that time. With Ichi, he had suddenly found himself shoved inside a sort of cylinder of hot flesh. He'd been taken by surprise, having supposed that women were soft. She'd felt so muscular. It had been like being sucked on inside a creature's mouth. One time when he was little, a calf had sucked on his finger, latching on and vigorously working its thick tongue. Ichi had been like that.

Otoku's carping, angry voice was partly to blame, but since then, Takezo had been oddly scared of Ichi. When he saw her, the face of that calf with a ring in its nose loomed before him.

They entered a back alley crowded on both sides with narrow, two-story establishments. Ichi had never been here before. She pricked up her ears. For some reason, there was the sound of a baby crying. Or had she imagined it? No, somewhere an infant was crying faintly. Scuffed sandals lay scattered in dirt-floor entrances, front doors were wide open for all to see, and laundry flapped in the breeze at the ends of narrow lanes. Faded underskirts and men's worn-out drawers hung side by side, dripping wet.

They came to a signboard marked "Yoshidaya" and stood in front of the small brothel. By the threshold, a tiny pair of children's sandals lay overturned. Ichi and Takezo looked at each other. Peering inside the dim interior, they made out a staircase that apparently led straight up to rooms where prostitutes entertained clients. This arrangement was typical of lower-class establishments that didn't serve food and drink.

In the middle of the stairs sat two little girls around five or six years old, playing with dolls. They had laid out little cups and saucers; one clasped a doll to her chest, the other carried hers on her back. Ichi looked at them in astonishment, and they silently returned her gaze.

"Anybody home?" Ichi called. No answer. "Do you live here?" she asked, but the girls couldn't understand her speech and only stared, wide-eyed. "We're here for Nazuna. Go upstairs and call her for me, will you?"

"Mama'll scold us . . ."

Their mother must have put the second floor, where women plied their trade, off-limits.

The girls backed away, looking frightened, and then ran off bawling.

"What is it? What's going on?"

A pale woman with a headache plaster on her temple came out. She did not resemble a trainer or owner, much less a prostitute. She held an infant to her bony chest, the front of her kimono wide open.

Then she realized who they were and shouted for Nazuna. The next moment, Nazuna came running, carrying a cloth-wrapped bundle and wiping her wet hands on her kimono sleeve.

"Thank you," she said to the other woman. "I'll be off, then." She stepped down into the entryway and slipped on her sandals.

The woman holding the baby looked balefully at Ichi and Takezo. "She's still got a lot of work to do. See that you bring her right back."

Ichi and Takezo were only too glad to get away. What an awful place! Nazuna seemed to be working as both maid and prostitute. Or rather, the Yoshidaya made no distinction between the two.

"Why are you in a place like that?" Ichi asked.

"My pa got into debt." That was all Nazuna said.

The threesome went through the big gate and passed the guardhouse, then crossed the Shirakawa River. When they reached the other side, Nazuna turned and looked back. Ichi and Takezo did, too. Over there, where they lived, they felt as if they were living normal lives, but seen from here, their way of life was truly bizarre. Yet that world, too, was human and real, not some fantasy realm floating in the air.

"Hey, cow!" Ichi said to Takezo. "Over there, she and I are like worms. Even a guy like you is a pathetic worm." She spat on the bridge.

Takezo, looking miffed, started walking on again by himself. Then he turned and said, "I'm not a cow or a worm."

"Oh, listen! A big talker!" Ichi jeered.

Takezo's face turned red. "Humph. No point in telling this to a couple of prostitutes, but I learned to read and write and do sums, and one of these days I'll be manager of a big place!"

Ichi laughed out loud. "Manager of a brothel, eh? Whoop-de-do!" Still laughing, she grabbed Nazuna by the hand and took off. "The cow got mad, better run!"

Nazuna ran with her. Takezo followed them sullenly, his arms laden with fruit, scurrying as fast as he was able.

By the time they arrived at the villa in Nezu, it was well past noon. Murasaki came out to greet them, looking thinner than ever. She was breastfeeding, and her body gave off the faint, rather off-putting smell of milk. Well, you couldn't tend to an infant by sitting around looking pretty, Ichi reflected.

She presented Murasaki with the fruit and the package of Uji tea from Shinonome. In return, Murasaki shyly handed her some seaweed paste flavored with soy sauce that her parents had sent her. "Thank you so much, everyone." She lowered her head in gratitude.

An oiran seldom if ever lowered her head to anyone. She's really changed, thought Ichi.

The baby was lying asleep on a small red futon, fists up by its head.

"What a darling!" Nazuna exclaimed.

"Like a little bean," Ichi said.

Though only several days old, Murasaki's newborn baby had perfectly formed eyes, nose, and mouth. She was truly the daughter of an oiran. But who could her father be? Neither Mohei nor Tose nor Shinonome had asked, and Murasaki was not letting on. As a consummate professional, an oiran had to know the identity of her child's father. Yet Murasaki had opted to give birth to a fatherless child.

"What's her name?" Ichi asked.

Murasaki forced a faint smile. "I can't quite make up my mind. So for the time being, she has no name."

"No name! Poor thing!" Nazuna tittered.

"So you've got no name, eh?" As Ichi spoke, the baby opened its eyes wide.

"I think she heard you," said Nazuna.

The baby's eyes were the clear, light blue of the heavens, with pupils like moist black jewels. Those pupils were trained steadily on Ichi, as if to say, *I'm me. I'm me, myself. Do you see?*

Ichi returned her gaze. *You haven't even got a name! What are you talking about?*

This infant without a father or a name continued to gaze at Ichi with dark, shining eyes, until Ichi grew afraid and looked away.

"The manager said to tell you to come back soon," Ichi said.

“Yes, I will, after the rainy season.” Murasaki spoke without enthusiasm.

Would she really come back? Or, as Shinonome suspected, would she do no such thing? If she did come back, a foster mother would have to be found. The baby would be fatherless *and* motherless.

Sushi was served. The sea was nearby, the seafood fresh. Ichi and Nazuna both recalled the taste of fish back home. Takezo was eating his lunch in the anteroom, they were told.

Soon after that, they left.

“When you come back, I’ll help carry your things,” Ichi said.

Murasaki smiled without answering.

Ichi suddenly wondered what Murasaki’s real name was. Then she remembered that Shinonome had once said it was Itoko. Murasaki’s family were weavers, so they had given her a name using the character *ito*, “thread.” What sort of life had she led before being sold? What was her family like? Ichi realized she knew nothing about Murasaki.

Ichi, Nazuna, and Takezo left the village of Nezu and trudged on, heading back the way they had come.

Ichi recalled the time before, when she had come with Shinonome. On the way back, right about here her lower abdomen had begun to feel bloated. The little bag inside her had been full, gasping for relief. Blood had gushed out. Some unknown place inside her had given the order, and out it had come. But she no longer feared this happening. She had practiced just as Shinonome had taught her to and could now control her menstrual flow at will.

The town was still far off. They walked along a high riverbank.

Nazuna began to fidget.

"What's wrong?" Takezo called out from behind.

"My insides hurt."

"Your insides?"

Any reference to a woman's physical complaints left Takezo at a loss. He didn't know what to do.

"It's her red silk," Ichi said.

"Her what?"

"You know, a woman's monthly period."

Nazuna clutched her abdomen and crouched down at the side of the road.

"Something about this place makes a woman's period come on," said Ichi. "It's weird. Nezu is a jinx for red silk."

Takezo looked disturbed. Two valuable women had been entrusted to him. Although nowhere near as valuable as an oiran, even a cheap prostitute was like a wallet filled with money. He had to get them back safely.

"What do you want me to do? Carry you to a doctor?"

Nazuna shook her head, her head bent as she bore the pain.

"A doctor can't help," Ichi said.

"I'll just go down by the river for a minute," said Nazuna.

She stood up unsteadily. A path led down to the stream below. She started walking in that direction, holding her abdomen.

"Will you be okay by yourself?" Ichi asked.

"I'll be fine. Don't come. And don't watch!"

Ichi groped inside her kimono sleeve for the small cloth bag containing a rolled-up rag that she carried with her in case of emergency. She handed it to Nazuna. Nazuna descended the steep grassy embankment. Along the way she turned and said desperately, "Don't watch!"

The look on her face petrified them.

Nazuna walked downhill through the grass, the sound of her footsteps growing faint.

Ichi and Takezo looked at each other.

"Is she all right?" he wondered aloud.

Nazuna took forever. Ichi worried that she might have collapsed, but when Takezo started off after her, she tried to stop him.

"It's my job!" He shook her off and darted down the path that Nazuna had taken. A manservant's number one job was to watch over the prostitutes to protect them and also to keep them from running away. A responsibility too heavy for a boy of seventeen.

"Nazuna!" he called, softly and fearfully. He strained his ears, listening to the sound of the river's current, then let out a sudden shout: "Don't tell me you've escaped!"

If that were the case, they would go after her. Even if she slipped past him, other pursuers would take over. Professionals. What happened when they caught their prey, he had never seen. Whether the captured women lived or died, he didn't know. Nobody ever spoke of that.

Few peered willingly into the darkness.

At the foot of the embankment, alongside the river, there was a walkway constructed of wood planks. From there Takezo stood and inspected the river end to end. The sparkling surface of the water bore no sign of any human form. He remembered playing by a river like this when he was a little boy, catching mud snails. A dozen years had passed like a dream, and now here he stood by this other river, terrified.

Ichi came sliding down the embankment to join him.

Takezo walked along the river. Ahead just a ways was a slight break in the embankment where a branch of the river flowed. If you went across on stepping-stones, a path led to the far bank.

"I'll go after her. You go back and tell them what happened!" Takezo started to run but caught himself, his feet in a tangle, and grabbed Ichi roughly by the arm. This one might take it into her head to run away, too. "No, come with me. We'll look together!"

He tugged on Ichi so hard that she nearly fell over. They ran like mad, Takezo never releasing his grip.

That evening when Ichi and Takezo returned to the Shinonome covered in sweat and dust, Saito, old Otoku, and Tose were sitting in the entrance, waiting. Seated a short distance away, holding a baby, was the woman from the Yoshidaya. All four looked darkly at Ichi and Takezo.

The Yoshidaya woman grabbed Takezo and shook him, demanding to know what had become of Nazuna.

"She ran away."

Saito stood up and punched Takezo. He hit him so hard that the boy went flying all the way to the front door. Ichi ran over to where Takezo lay prone and shielded his body with hers.

"Wait! There was nothin' he could do!"

The Yoshidaya woman screamed, "You'll pay for this! I want money! Nazuna was my best worker!"

Her only worker, to be accurate. Since she had no other employees, losing Nazuna left her desperate.

That same evening the Yoshidaya woman set off for the association office, accompanied by Saito, and filed for reimbursement of the loss incurred by Nazuna's disappearance. When a prostitute absconded, the brothel owner was entitled to be repaid the amount invested in her purchase. Charges were filed against the missing woman and reported to associations around the country, as well as to the local police.

But nothing further was ever heard of Nazuna.

Some ten days later, a wanted notice ran in the association publication, *Joko shimbun*. A newspaper in name only, it was a circular passed around in the licensed quarter. The notice read as follows:

> On June 20 Yoshida Mitsu, owner of the Yoshidaya, filed a claim for damages against Sakihama Sue, 18, originally of Kanezaki Hamaka 2537, Chikuzen, who fled on June 19.
>
> Height: just over 4 ft.
>
> Weight: just over 100 lbs.
>
> Speaks with a Chikuzen accent; thin eyebrows; small eyes; missing one upper left molar; mole on left earlobe; taciturn by nature.

The stern printed text seemed to refer to someone else, not Nazuna. Her real name, "Sakihama Sue," looked cold, like that of a total stranger. But Nazuna had indeed disappeared from the licensed quarter. Shinonome told Ichi that she must not speak of the missing girl to Murasaki.

"Did Murasaki really recognize Nazuna, do you think?" Shinonome blew a stream of smoke from her long pipe.

Ichi looked up in surprise. Come to think of it, Murasaki hadn't said anything of particular note to Nazuna, and Nazuna hadn't addressed the oiran, either. She had simply stayed quietly by Ichi's side. But neither had Murasaki looked at Nazuna curiously and asked, "Who's this?" Perhaps she'd assumed Nazuna came along to keep Ichi company.

"Even if Murasaki did find her presence strange, an oiran would never say so aloud," Shinonome said. A woman standing at the apex of her sex would not say or do anything to wound those below. She would treat everyone the same.

"Don't *you* remember Nazuna?" Ichi asked.

Shinonome's laugh rang out, chiming like bells. "I never even saw her face. How could I remember someone I've never seen?"

The white smoke from her pipe drifted in front of Ichi like the clouds of paradise.

One morning it rained hard. Few braved such weather to come to school, so Tetsuko wrote out a model for Kogin and Kikumaru to copy. Then, after an absence of more than ten days, in came Ichi. Outside was the sound of thunder, and the rain was coming down in sheets.

Ichi wiped her feet dry in the corner and then slunk to her seat like a cat who had just been scolded.

"Good morning, teacher."

"Good morning to you. We are practicing calligraphy this morning."

"No, I want to write in my journal."

The girl had a mind of her own. Tetsuko smiled and, as usual, let her do as she pleased. Ichi took out paper, ground some ink, and picked up her brush. She sat hunched over the desk. Something must be eating at her again, thought Tetsuko. Things eat away at her, small though she is.

Ichi thought and thought before starting to write.

July 1　Heavy rain　Aoi Ichi

My friend escaped.
Now shes a wanted woman.
I dont know where she went.
The day after she disappeared
a pair of little girls started coming
in front of the place where I work.
Give her back! they shout.
Give us back our big sister!
On rainy days Give her back!
On fine days Give her back!
They bring their dolls and stand out front
　　shouting.

I cant go to the bath.
Cant go to school.
Im going to disappear for a while too.
Sorry for missing school.

Ichi laid the paper on Tetsuko's desk and rushed back into the rain. Thunder rumbled as if in pursuit.

Not Human

Tonight, Shinonome's client was the founder of a private railroad company. A longtime regular, he was very old. After an all-hands-on-deck banquet, she led him gently into her bedchamber, where she would simply cradle him in her arms as he slept.

Ichi and Tamagiku retired to their little room and crawled onto futons laid out side by side. On a night like this, Shinonome seemed to Ichi more than ever like a grand ship of comfort and repose like the Pure Land might offer, gliding off on the night sea with a burst of gaiety. Although she spent more time with Shinonome than she did with anyone else, sometimes the oiran seemed to her less like a human being than a phantasmagorical creature. Sometimes she was Kannon, the goddess of mercy, and other times she was the female sex itself, towering like an enormous rock.

Ichi's and Tamagiku's eyes were wide open in the

darkness. Having just come from the bright, boisterous banquet room, neither of them was sleepy. Ichi thought of Murasaki, sleeping with her baby in Nezu. She turned her face toward Tamagiku.

"I've been thinking."

"What about?" Tamagiku, lying on her back, answered with little interest.

"What happens if I get pregnant?"

Tamagiku let out a snort of laughter. "Pregnant? You?" She laughed again.

Ichi pouted. "I'm a woman. I could get pregnant."

Tamagiku giggled. "Oh, absolutely. Sure you could. But not for long. If you're pregnant, you can't work. Either the mother dies or the baby does. Not much choice there."

So that was that. Ichi had once seen Otoku come running to drag a pale young woman off to the futon storage room. The young woman had been miserable with morning sickness.

"Otoku uses a teacup to push medicine into the mother's mouth down below, and that's the end of it. The baby dissolves and comes out." Tamagiku spoke of this hair-raising matter in a normal voice.

"What about just having the baby?"

"Forget it. Ordinary prostitutes can't take time off until their contract is up. If you don't want Otoku doing that to you, don't get pregnant."

“What about a prostitute who’s not ordinary?”

“An oiran, you mean? I suppose an oiran can, but it wouldn’t be a very happy thing for her.” Tamagiku’s tone was dark. “For an oiran to have a baby is beyond the pale. She’s a beautiful blossom; she’s not supposed to have anything to do with childbirth. They’d let her go through with the pregnancy, though, just to avoid any harm coming to a body so beautiful. If the baby’s a girl and takes after her mother, they can always turn her into another oiran when she grows up.”

A baby girl would return to the brothel from foster care at age seven or eight.

“But for an oiran to conceive the child of a client means he’s bested her. The queen of women defeated by an ordinary man. It’s a huge loss of face.”

Ichi was impressed. Though still a prepubescent child, Tamagiku grasped the subtleties of life in a brothel better than an adult.

“Clients come to see an oiran because they want to sleep with a queen. That’s why they pay those ridiculous sums of money.”

“So you’re saying Murasaki is a loser, a failure as an oiran?”

“’Fraid so.” Tamagiku giggled again. The light was out, so Ichi couldn’t see her face.

“Then why do they want her back?” It made no sense.

Murasaki hadn't yet said definitely that she *would* return. She must be turning it over in her mind, unable to decide. An oiran, being subject to rigid constraints, couldn't bear just anybody's child. The father had to be one of her favored clients. The handful of local men qualified to become the client of an oiran were titans of the local rail, shipping, and fishing industries. Murasaki's failure to reveal the father's name might mean she didn't want him redeeming her debt. Or perhaps he wanted his name kept out of it for reasons of his own. In any case, for her to make her way in the world with a small child in tow would be no small feat. Out there, an oiran was just another woman.

On the other hand, if she did return to the Shinonome, she'd find her value as an oiran diminished. Never again would she measure up to Shinonome.

"They say just one in a thousand women can be an oiran, if that." Tamagiku sounded forlorn. She herself was being groomed to become an oiran one day. "Having babies is something any ordinary woman can do. That's not what an oiran's patrons are after."

"Which is what?"

Tamagiku let out a long breath. "I don't know yet. But it has to be something extraordinary, not what just anyone could provide. If all they wanted was someone to be nice in an ordinary way, they've always got their missus at home. Or their mistress."

This made sense.

"I can't say exactly what it is men are after, but I have a feeling we should be able to tell by looking at our oiran. So Kojika, tell me, how is Shinonome different from an ordinary woman?"

"Hmm . . ."

Shinonome was courageous, strong-willed, proud, extravagant, and self-indulgent; sometimes mean, sometimes nice; also gentle, intelligent, and highly intuitive, with a tongue that could be sharp or smooth. The more Ichi thought about it, the less she knew what to make of Shinonome. The oiran was formidable.

"I dunno."

"Maybe that's it. Maybe it's her mystery that appeals to men."

Once again, Ichi found Tamagiku to be eerily perceptive. "You think Murasaki's ever coming back?"

"I wonder. Giving up her baby would be painful, but if she left here and tried to support the two of them by herself, she'd have a hard time."

And yet amas made their living from the sea, Ichi thought, and farmers lived off the land.

She sensed that Tamagiku had turned her head to face her. The girl's voice sounded closer in the darkness.

"The master's come up with a plan. He's going to let Murasaki bring her baby back with her."

"What! How can she?"

"He hasn't said anything to her yet. The only ones who know are the mistress, and Saito, and Shinonome."

And you, because you eavesdropped, Ichi thought.

"It's a huge gamble for him," Tamagiku went on. "It means she'll have the baby with her at banquets, and when she goes on promenade the wet nurse will follow her, holding the baby in her arms. The master has thought it all through."

Ichi was now wide awake. "I've never heard of an oiran like that."

"There's been one before, though."

According to Tamagiku, long ago in old Edo, at the most prestigious brothel in the Yoshiwara pleasure district there had been a series of oirans named Takao. One of them, whether Takao I or a successor Tamagiku didn't know, was called Childbearing Takao.

"She heard that a former client of hers had suffered a reversal of fortune."

"A reversal of fortune?"

"Financial ruin. So she invited him to the brothel at her own expense and ended up getting pregnant. After the baby was born, she kept it with her when receiving clients, and during the oiran procession she had the wet nurse follow her, carrying the baby. This made a huge impression on people and earned her the name Childbearing Takao. She became more famous than ever. People said she was an oiran for all time, a woman for all time."

"So now our Murasaki will be Childbearing Murasaki."

"People will be astonished, won't they?"

That might not be all, Ichi thought. They might be appalled and turn her into a laughingstock. What then?

"It all comes down to her looks," Tamagiku said quietly.

Though Ichi herself was not directly affected, the future of an oiran who had been kind to her hung in the balance. She stared into the darkness.

Soon the time came to present the baby at a nearby Shinto shrine. Tose set out for Nezu early one morning by rickshaw. After accompanying the mother and child to the shrine, she came back early in the afternoon. The baby's name, she reported, was Shino.

After changing her clothes, Tose climbed upstairs to Shinonome's room, mopping perspiration off her forehead.

"When is Murasaki coming back?" This question was at the front of Shinonome's mind.

"She says she wants to nurse the baby herself for the first three months."

"Nearly two months more . . ."

The longer Murasaki nursed her child, the more her body would waste away. Tose was beside herself with worry. If only Murasaki would put the baby out to nurse!

"She's gotten awfully thin, so I took her some soft-shell turtle meat."

Tose didn't care a fig about the baby. She wanted their strongbox to come back in good health and begin earning again.

"Anyway," Tose concluded, "that's where things stand, so you'll have to carry on alone a bit longer."

"I have little choice . . ."

"By the way," Tose said, lowering her voice, "I stopped by the association on the way back and heard some disturbing news. Four more girls have disappeared. They've disappeared from the Izumiya and the Gessho, yesterday and the day before."

Shinonome glanced at Ichi, who was cleaning. "They ran away?"

"Jumped into the river and swam across."

Nazuna's escape was still recent. Sometimes these things happened in clusters. All four girls had been purchased from fishing villages on the islands of Amakusa, off the west coast of Kyushu. They were swimmers, and the rainy season having ended, the current of the river was slack.

"That makes eight runaways since the first of this month." Tose ticked them off on her fingers. "What on earth is going on?"

Ichi pricked up her ears as she polished the pillar in

the alcove. She heard Shinonome murmur, "They have no notion of the consequences."

Escapees assumed that as long as they got away, all would be well, but because they were reneging on their debt, their families faced harsh repercussions. A family poor enough to sell a daughter into prostitution naturally lacked the means to pay off the debt. If there were a younger brother, he would go work for the brothel, and if there were a younger sister, she, too, would be taken like her sister before her. The wheel of misery spun around and around.

"They issued wanted notices right away and sent them all around the country." Tose sounded weary.

"It's too bad, but what else can they do?"

Once flyers containing their descriptions were circulated nationwide, runaways had no place to hide. To avoid detection, they ended up drifting to brothels outside the association, those known as "hells." What Tose couldn't understand was why there would be a run of these suicidal escape attempts now. She had the disquieting sense that prostitutes throughout the licensed quarter were secretly planning their getaways. Nothing like this had ever happened before. Perhaps someone was exerting influence behind the scenes, but who? She couldn't think of anyone capable of such machinations. Unless . . .

"Do you suppose it's the Christian Salvation Army, stirring them up behind our backs?"

Lately, the Salvation Army had been stepping up its activities in the vicinity with the avowed goal of helping people and reforming society.

Shinonome looked skeptical. "The Salvation Army couldn't possibly help them escape so openly. If they did, their headquarters would come under police investigation, and that would be the end of their proselytizing. And anyway, the Salvation Army is in no position to take on the girls' debts."

As she polished the wooden pillar, Ichi pictured the faces of the little girls from the Yoshidaya who'd been making such pests of themselves. They must have given up or gotten tired, for they hadn't been around the last few days.

Give her back!

Nazuna had been the Yoshidaya's cash cow. The proprietress of the Yoshidaya had two little girls and a baby besides, so without Nazuna, they really needed money. The little girls had come by to express their mother's rage. Little did they know that their family had been sucking Nazuna dry.

Give her back!

The dirty little ragamuffins. Good riddance.

•

Tetsuko arrived at the Female Industrial School at her usual time one morning to find a line of prostitutes stretching beyond the gate. Today was the first day of the monthly medical checkup. The line began in the medical office and wound past the sewing room, around the corner, and down the hall beyond Tetsuko's classroom. She saw Ichi and Kogin in line waiting their turn.

Ichi spotted Tetsuko and called out to her, "At this rate, it'll take us all morning!"

A handful of local gynecologists conducted the examinations, working from morning to night over several days. The process was nothing like the private examinations conducted in Shinonome's apartment by a professor from Kyushu Imperial University. All day long, women spread their legs and closed them, spread their legs and closed them, displaying the ravages of sexually transmitted diseases in a dizzying array: roseola, papules, cockscomb ulcers, cauliflower warts, redness, sores, ulceration, abscesses. Why did ailments on a woman's lower body resemble flowers? Poisonous flowers in gruesome colors that blossomed on flesh in the dark.

Those found to be ailing were prescribed disinfectant, medicine, and rest. For a while, anyway, they could take a break from work, for which they thanked God, the Female Industrial School, and the doctors. But not working meant not earning, so the noose only tightened more.

Tetsuko opened the door to the peach-blossom classroom, opened the windows to freshen the air, and put on her reading glasses. She took out a stack of compositions from the day before and laid it on her desk. Ichi's was on top. Lately her lettering, which was like the slime trails of sea slugs, had grown a little more uniform.

July 18 Sunny Aoi Ichi
Nazuna of the Yoshidaya still hasnt turned up.
Yesterday I heard the mistress and Saito talking downstairs.
Nazuna is from a seaside village.
The Yoshidaya sent a debt collector there.
He said her family had no tatamis or futons or lamps.
The floor was busted and they used a straw mat for a door.
Her pa had straggly hair
her ma had on only a ragged underskirt
her little brother had a runny nose
her grandpa was bedridden
her granny was blind
and the dog was mangy.
They all stared in surprise, mouths open, he said.

Tetsuko held the back of her hand to her forehead and closed her eyes, visualizing life in an impoverished fishing village. Nazuna's hometown was in northern Kyushu. Because of the ocean currents, winters there were freezing, unlike here on the balmy southern end of Kyushu, and life was harsh. The Yoshidaya had hired a debt collector to go there, but he'd been unable to recover any of the money owed.

When Tetsuko was growing up, her father's stipend had been meager, but their house had had tatamis, lamps, and futons. Ichi's account reminded her of a debt collector's report filed after the disappearance of a previous member of the peach-blossom class, a young woman named Yoshino:

> I set out for her hometown of Miyazaki and searched in the mountains until I found her family home. Their sole possessions consisted of a broken cooking pan, an old cooking stove, three ragged straw mats, and a pair of old futons resembling torn seaweed that had washed ashore. The house itself struck me as having no value, not worth the trouble of taking it apart board by board to sell. I used up the travel allowance without recovering a cent of the money owed.

The desperate poverty of the families of girls sold into prostitution in the quarter was beyond Tetsuko's imagination.

Yet if somehow one of those dirt-poor families did manage to scrape together enough money to reimburse the brothel where they had sold their daughter, the police would never bother her again. Strange as it may seem, the Prostitute Liberation Law of 1872 had outlawed human trafficking, enslavement, and abusive contracts. The law declared such practices a violation of human rights, emancipating all prostitutes, geishas, and bonded laborers.

That same month had seen the proclamation of what was popularly referred to as the Livestock Emancipation Law because of its bizarre phrasing.

> Prostitutes and geishas have lost their human rights and are no different from livestock. No one would expect an animal to pay back the price of its purchase. In the same way, prostitutes and geishas should not be required to pay what they owe to the purchasing establishment.

These opening lines, dismissing prostitutes as not humans but animals, had shocked and angered Tetsuko. Furthermore, while this law had forbidden human trafficking, it by no means ended prostitution. Prostitutes were allowed to rent places where they could conduct their business, a glaring loophole that enabled brothels to flourish.

The law had been revamped in 1900, three years before Ichi was sold to the Shinonome, granting prostitutes the right, in principle, to quit the business if they wished. This development was the fruit of efforts by the Salvation Army, the United Church of Christ in Japan, and the women's rights movement.

Brothel owners, however, were not content to let valuable workers simply walk away. As a countermove, they rewarded high-earning prostitutes with twice-yearly bonuses, depositing the funds in bank accounts to help the women prepare for life after their contracts expired. In addition, they established schools in the licensed quarters to provide prostitutes with a general education.

While these changes marked great progress in the history of the licensed quarters, prostitutes were prevented from running away by an upswing in intimidation, threats, violence, surveillance, and searches. When one of them did disappear, an agent was sent off to collect from her parents whatever remained of the money from her sale. These measures had the desired effect, causing a steep drop in the number of runaways, as most women chose to accept their lot rather than subject their parents to harassment from debt collectors. Besides, they had no idea how to make a living outside the licensed quarter.

Inside the quarter, there were some rules. Outside, there were none at all. Leaving meant stepping into hell, but staying was another kind of hell. Each woman had to decide for herself which hell to choose.

The buzz of conversation in the hallway outside the classroom was noisier than ever. The line kept getting longer. As there were only three or four doctors for over eight hundred girls, this gridlock was no surprise. Finally, with evening approaching and the need to prepare for clients more pressing, the end of the line began to break up as some gave up and left.

Tetsuko removed her glasses and laid them on the desk.

She was upset with Fukuzawa Yukichi. His treatise *New Greater Learning for Women*, which had begun serialization in *Jiji Shimpo* two years before the founding of the Female Industrial School, had thrilled her with its progressive spirit. In his discussion of women's education, Yukichi had recommended that girls receive the same physical education as men and declared physics—science—to be the foundation of all learning.

Well-bred young women studied classics of Japanese literature, including thirty-one-syllable waka poetry, but Yukichi, while acknowledging the literary beauty of such works, judged them inappropriate for young minds—not only because the classics were short on scientific thinking but also because they were corrupting, depraved, and impure, unworthy of veneration. He saw even Murasaki Shikibu and Sei Shonagon as wanton and indecent, putting them on the same plane as prostitutes. When she first encountered that audacious appraisal, Tetsuko had felt a pleasure like that of casting off an old kimono.

However, as the serialization continued and she read further, she was left aghast at the author's concepts of equality and justice. They made her skin crawl. He showered equal love only on the well-born of her sex. No matter how highly educated and well read a woman might be, no matter how broad her intellect and versatile her talents, if she did not possess refinement, he said, she did not deserve to be called a proper lady.

The example Yukichi gave of "depraved and vulgar" women were those employed in red-light districts:

> Vulgar females bedeck themselves in costumes to sing and dance with unseemly familiarity before drunken clients, talking nonsense and showing no discretion. No one who saw this spectacle could call such a woman anything but a slut.

On reading this passage, Tetsuko was filled with rage and sorrow. The essay went on to say that while some such women were doubtless merely lacking in judgment and didn't know any better, they, too, deserved to be called sluts. A few lines later, Yukichi went further:

> [Women working in the licensed quarters] will be excluded from discussion because they are not human to begin with.

This sentence tore at Tetsuko's heart. The words "not human" could refer to a person who did not display basic human decency or to a beast. This was no different from the thinking in the purely cosmetic Livestock Emancipation Law issued by the Ministry of Justice.

Elsewhere Yukichi wrote that sometimes concubines and geishas did "rise from the gutter and make something of themselves" by marrying into a good family. However, such women remained "disgraceful creatures" not fit for the company of "fine ladies." Though they "amply deserved to be despised," a lady of good breeding must not let her feelings show.

> To look down on such a woman with open contempt, as if to say "I am pure and you are soiled; I am high and you are low," serves only to lower one's own dignity.

Why was a woman of good family "pure" and one who had emerged from the licensed quarter "soiled"? Why was a lady "high" and a former prostitute "low"? As her eyes traced the words on the page, Tetsuko was horrified to discover the reality of the man who had made the famous declaration "Heaven does not create one person above another."

The essay concluded with this advice:

> The compassionate response is to pity her privately for her lack of education and her lack of common decency.

What egotistical compassion!

Tetsuko could not help thinking of her friend Matsuhashi Takeko, who, like her, had been sold into prostitution long ago. While working in the Matsuei in Tokyo's Yoshiwara district, Takeko had read book after book and also had acquired the full array of usual feminine accomplishments. After a young man with a degree in science from Tokyo Imperial University fell in love with her, they had married and gone off to live in Berlin, Germany. If Fukuzawa Yukichi ran into her there, how would he greet her? He himself was from a lower-class samurai family, Tetsuko had heard. Those in the higher echelons are pure, distinguished, and noble; those in the lower echelons are soiled, degenerate, and contemptible. This horrendous philosophy of inequality and injustice must be a product of Yukichi's own low standing in the samurai class.

The classroom door rattled, then opened a crack. A dark eye regarded Tetsuko, interrupting her musings.

"Come in."

The door slid all the way open, and in came Ichi.

"Are you finished? How did it go?"

"I'm okay!" Ichi said. "Nothing's wrong with me!"

What a relief! It was the same every month. Tetsuko could not breathe easy until she heard those words.

In August, Tose set out again for the villa in Nezu. She was going ostensibly to check on the progress of mother and child, but her real aim was to persuade Murasaki to return quickly to the Shinonome. Of course, the oiran wouldn't have to resume work right away. The main thing was to let her clients know that she was back.

Early that afternoon Tose returned in high spirits, bearing news that set the office buzzing with excitement. As planned, in her conversation with Murasaki she had brought up the topic of Childbearing Takao.

"She was troubled about putting the baby out to nurse and couldn't decide what to do, but when I said, 'Both of you come on back!' she looked flabbergasted. Her jaw dropped."

"I'll bet it did," said Saito.

"I told her, 'You'll be this generation's Childbearing Takao!' Her eyes popped, and tears streamed down her face."

Tose's approach had succeeded.

With the question mark hanging over her return now removed, the sooner Murasaki came back with her baby, the better. They wouldn't pressure her to sleep with clients; unlike ordinary prostitutes, an oiran rarely took clients to bed, anyway. She wouldn't be rushed into resuming work so soon after giving birth. Before anything else, she needed to be introduced as Childbearing Murasaki.

Saito leaned forward eagerly as they made plans.

Several days later, Mohei went to Nezu to work out the details. It was decided that mother and child would arrive at the end of August, when the midsummer Bon festivities would be over and the weather would have cooled off.

The next morning, the news spread quickly through the Shinonome. All anyone could talk about was Murasaki and her baby. There was no more bizarre combination than a prostitute and a baby. Looking for a baby in a brothel was like going to the sea to find the mountains, or to the mountains to find the sea. What could be sillier than a prostitute with a baby?

The baby at the Yoshidaya belonged to the brothel's mistress, which was equally unusual. No wonder Ichi had stared.

And now Murasaki was going to bring back one of those rare creatures. Not surreptitiously, either, but openly for all to see. She would show the baby to her clients and take it with her on parade. When word spread that the baby was a girl and looked exactly like her mother, the whole quarter lit up.

Mohei, concerned about Murasaki going up and down the stairs with an infant in her arms, prepared new quarters for her in a small detached house. A carpenter built a covered area in back where the baby's laundry could hang to dry even when it rained. Tose, meanwhile, set to work finding a wet nurse and helper for the oiran and her baby.

"I'm a good babysitter!" Ichi went to Tose to volunteer her services but received a quick scolding: "Never mind that, you just tend to your customers!" Ichi shrugged and flinched. In Tose's lap was an infant's half-sewn undershirt.

Upstairs, Ichi found Shinonome staring out the window with the tip of her writing brush in her mouth. Her haiku notebook lay open on the low writing desk at her side.

"I've never tried to write a haiku about a baby before. It's harder than I thought." Shinonome took up her brush and smoothly wrote out a haiku in an elegant hand:

Shadowy water
where the water lilies bloom—
the newborn returns

Peering over her shoulder, Ichi wondered why she had referred to the baby as “the newborn.” “Baby” sounded cute to her, but “newborn” made her think of that tiny, sleek creature she had seen in Nezu.

After the physical examinations ended, the Female Industrial School regained its former tranquility. The number of students in the peach-blossom class had swelled to an even dozen, and one received bad news. A nineteen-year-old from the mountains of Miyazaki tested positive for gonorrhea. Fortunately, the disease was in the early stage, and treatment began immediately.

The news that Murasaki of the Shinonome was soon to return with her baby reached Tetsuko’s ears as well. Perhaps that was why Ichi’s face was so animated, she thought.

Ichi bent intently over her desk, scribbling, and then handed the paper to Tetsuko with vigor.

August 8 Rainy, then sunny Aoi Ichi
Murasaki is going to come back with her baby.
Everyone is happy about it.
Shinonome wrote a haiku.

Shadowy water
where the water lilies bloom—
the newborn returns.

The baby in Shinonome's haiku isnt cute.
I wrote my own haiku.

So far from home
the first star I see
is the baby.

Ma'am, you write a haiku for the baby, too, please.

In Shinonome's haiku, the darkness of water on which water lilies floated created a striking visual image. The baby had emerged from dark amniotic fluid in its mother's womb. The poem seemed to be about a child whose birth brought little joy.

Ichi's baby, however, was a star child, innocent and pure. The first star of evening, outshining all the rest. By "home" she must mean her home island of Iojima, far off in the southern seas. Farther away even than the stars. Tetsuko had never read a haiku by Ichi before.

When class ended and Ichi started to leave, Tetsuko handed her a folded sheet of writing paper and told her to give it to Shinonome.

Later that afternoon, as Shinonome was putting on her makeup in preparation for the evening ahead, Ichi slipped something into her hand. It was from Tetsuko; Shinonome recognized the handwriting. When she unfolded the sheet of paper she found these lines, written with grace and economy, drawing on the ancient tale of an infant princess found inside a stalk of bamboo:

Young bamboo—
from the stalk emerged
a tiny princess.

How very odd it must be to have a stranger's baby.

Tetsuko

Shinonome studied the paper for a while before putting it away in her desk drawer, looking thoughtful.

August 13, the Bon holiday honoring the dead, was a grand festival day in the licensed quarter. Geishas joined in the spirited dancing on Nakamise Avenue, and colorful lanterns hung from the eaves of the brothels lining the street, inscribed with the names of famous oirans and courtesans of bygone days.

Mohei and Tose greeted their best clients that day, dropping hints that Murasaki and her baby would return at the end of the month. Any man rich enough to afford the company of an oiran of course knew the story of Childbearing Takao. When they heard the news, men slapped their knees with pleasure and leaned forward to hear more. Rumors of the coming debut of Childbearing Murasaki began to circulate well before the oiran's return.

The date of the return was set for August 28, and the time of day was also agreed on. The townspeople were restless, eager to see the sight for themselves. Then, a week before the big day, a letter arrived from Murasaki in Nezu that sent the Shinonome management into a frenzy.

At this late date, Murasaki had changed her mind. She wrote that she would not be returning after all. Instead, she and her baby would move away. Mohei and Tose immediately summoned a pair of rickshaws and raced to Nezu. They appealed to Murasaki, but her mind was firmly set. She had no desire to be compared to the grand Childbearing Takao of yore, she said. All she wanted was to live a quiet life raising her daughter.

She said she would leave unassisted. According to the law passed just four years earlier, prostitutes were free to cease working as long as they paid their debt, which Murasaki could easily afford to do. She even offered to add on a generous amount in apology for the trouble she had caused.

In the end, Mohei gave up.

On the morning of August 28, Murasaki quietly left the Nezu villa by rickshaw with her child and disappeared. Mohei and Tose were there to see her off, along with Saito, Otoku, and Shinonome.

By coincidence, at dawn that day three more young women escaped the licensed quarter by diving into the Shirakawa River and swimming to the far bank. They, too, were the daughters of fishermen in the Amakusa islands. Their debts remained virtually intact. Pursuers went on the hunt for them, and debt collectors went to their parents' homes.

One rainy afternoon, Ichi gently deposited a sheet of paper on Tetsuko's desk and left.

August 30 Drizzle Aoi Ichi
Murasaki went away somewhere.
Her baby did, too.
It feels like a dream.

Shokkichi the Rat

"This month we have a lot of newcomers. Your rooms will be crowded for the time being, but please be patient." Saito the manager had gathered all the girls of the Shinonome for this announcement.

Fifteen shabbily dressed young girls sat hunched by the office on the first floor, weary and dirty from travel. By the look of it, some had cried themselves to sleep every night since leaving home. None of them had the rosy cheeks of youth; they drooped like withered leaves.

The newcomers seemed shaken, having just been subjected to Mohei's curt physical examination. From the back of the room, Ichi craned her neck to get a better look. Some faces were guileless and round, others were oval and would take nicely to makeup, still others were square or strong-jawed. Some were dark, some fair, some pale and delicate. The girls might be alike in their misery, but their looks were as varied as could be.

Register in hand, Saito began to introduce the

newcomers by reading their names aloud. He omitted their places of origin and birth names, saying only the work name each had been assigned. The girls responded timidly as their names were called, sometimes choking back tears. All of them had learned the new name necessary for their new life.

"Kazuki."

"Yubune."

"Tachibana."

"Kaede."

"Otome."

"Natsuno."

"Sammaru."

"Tomoe."

"Katsura."

"Yugiri."

"Kikuya."

"Akari."

"Miyoji."

"Hanataro."

"Umeyakko."

The names were romantic and alluring, capable of arousing male desire. When the girls heard their new names spoken aloud, they hesitated, unused to their new identities. The assigned names served to settle their owners in this new life. What anyone might think of her new name was of no significance. None of the girls could read or write, and so the characters their names were written with meant nothing to them.

As prostitutes in the Shinonome came and went, work names were recycled endlessly, circulating like invisible name tags. A work name became available when its former owner left because her contract was up or else when she died of illness or some other cause, was caught escaping and was sold to a lower-class establishment, or successfully escaped, never to be found. Unlike futons and pillows, work names never wore out and could be used and reused over and over again.

Three of the assigned names belonged to girls who had recently escaped: Katsura and Hanataro the month before, and early this month, Otome. Usually no one got farther than the guardhouse at the big gate, but those three had somehow slipped through and vanished. In response, Mohei brought in more replacements than usual, from all over Kyushu. Nor was he the only owner expanding his workforce. The other seventy-odd brothels in the association were following suit.

The times were not prosperous. The shipyard strike in nearby Nagasaki, where hundreds of workers had banded together and gained a victory over their employer, had grown out of the stagnant economy. And if times were hard in the city, the countryside was even more impoverished. The price of a young girl had plunged to nearly half of what it used to be. No wonder the quarter was flooded with new faces, as houses of pleasure seized the chance to purchase new workers at bargain prices. Ichi heard that even the Yoshidaya had found a replacement for Nazuna.

The influx of new occupants made the Shinonome feel crowded. Ichi and the kamuro Tamagiku were joined in their small bedroom by Otome, a girl with an oval face, fair skin, and even features, whose training Shinonome would oversee, as she was doing with Ichi.

"Where're you from?" Ichi asked.

"Takeda."

Ichi had no idea where in Kyushu that might be.

On her first night, Otome wept softly. Ichi poked her head out of the covers and tried to console her.

"You're so pretty, you'll have lots of customers in no time. Men'll love you, and you'll wear pretty clothes and pay off your debt before you know it. Don't cry."

Otome had been facing the other way. Now she jerked her head around to face Ichi. "Are you happy here? Do those things satisfy you?"

"What! Don't talk like a know-it-all!" Incensed, Ichi clenched her fist, but Tamagiku spoke up from the futon next to hers.

"Kojika, life is hopeless in a place like this. Let her cry all she wants. You and I should go to sleep." Sounding like a wise old woman, she pulled the thin summer quilt over her head.

Otome clutched her pillow and sobbed in mortification.

Autumn breezes finally brought relief on morning walks to and from the bathhouse. Ichi walked along carrying a basin packed with her towel and a cloth bag of soft rice bran to cleanse her skin with. At every corner, she ran into girls she had never seen before, rubes whose eyebrows weren't properly shaved and whose faces and napes were covered in soft downy hair.

"Wherever you look, there's an unfamiliar face," remarked Kogin, walking beside her. "They all look so childish. Is that what we looked like, this time last year?" She seemed to be fondly remembering those days.

"No." Ichi shook her head. "We were a little better." She looked at Kogin, Kikumaru, and the rest, walking in the morning sunlight. They might lack the freshness of the new girls, but their polish made them more beautiful.

Girls in the quarter looked down on ordinary women as the amateurs they were, ignorant of the fine points of dressing and conducting oneself.

One role of low-ranking prostitutes like Ichi and her colleagues was to initiate new girls in the art of shaving their eyebrows and face; they also taught them to walk with their toes turned in.

But what did it mean to be loved by men?

Ichi was beginning to understand.

Some women were objects of men's love and some were not. Some women's faces and bodies were smooth, their deportment and carriage exquisite, others' not. Being loved by men wasn't everything in life, but Ichi now understood what kind of beauty men found irresistible.

When she ducked under the awning of the Asahi-yu, the air inside was heavy with the smells of women even at this early hour. Half of the women putting on or taking off their clothes, or standing around in various stages of undress, were new arrivals from the outside world.

A thought occurred to her. Maybe being loved by men meant that when a man's big hands caressed you everywhere, on your neck and your chest and your belly and your bottom, your body acquired a smooth polish.

She pondered this. That would explain the sleek silkiness of Kogin and Kikumaru. The girls in front of her, shedding their rough, worn-out undergarments and drying their drab, lusterless hair, had not yet known a man's touch.

Ichi slipped through the throng and slid open the door to the bath. Here, too, women's bodies were everywhere amid the steam.

Ichi washed and rinsed herself, then cautiously lowered herself into the tub, slipping in among the other bathers. They all soaked in the hot water together, their bodies pressed back to back and back to front. The firm, rough skin of a thigh rubbing up against hers reminded Ichi of the thighs of her older sister, with whom she used to share a bed back home on the island.

Her sister had the skin of a wild girl with the rough texture of cotton cloth; thighs that were heavy, cold, and dense; the muscles of an ama, almost masculine; and a body that was deeply bronzed, since she lived immersed in the sea and sunlight, except in the coldest time of year. Nineteen years old, she would never know a life where you washed yourself with rice bran.

My big sister.

Tears came to Ichi's eyes.

Then someone in the water called out, "Nazuna, I'm leaving," and Ichi looked around in surprise.

"Okay. I'll be along in a minute."

The response came from just behind her. She turned and saw a girl's wet face. There was a mark on one cheek where she had scratched a mosquito bite. The outer corners of her eyes turned up a bit. This was not the face of the Nazuna she knew. There was, of course, no reason to expect that the other girl would be here; after running off on the way back from Nezu, she was hardly likely to pop in here for a morning bath. This must be her replacement at the Yoshidaya.

Ichi raised a dripping hand and cupped the girl's

ear. "I'm Kojika from the Shinonome. I was friends with the other Nazuna, the one before you," she whispered.

"Friends" wasn't exactly right, but she didn't know what else to say.

Nazuna nodded and raised her own dripping hand to cup Ichi's ear. "I've been at the Yoshidaya since the day before yesterday. They call me Nazuna, but my real name is Kuroda Shige. I'm from Hakata." Her tone was brisk.

"Hakata?"

"You never heard of it?"

Ichi shook her head.

"It's one of the biggest cities in Kyushu, as big as Nagasaki. I was born there." She gave a bright smile. "What about you? Where're you from?" Her eyes were lively with interest.

"I'm from Iojima. South of Kagoshima."

"I know about it."

"You do? How?"

"The other new girl at the Yoshidaya is from there."

Ichi jumped up in the water. "What's her name?"

"Haruna."

"No, her real name!"

Few girls on the island were the right age to sell. A work name offered no clue. Ichi's heart pounded.

"Don't know. If you want to see her, she's right in there getting dressed." Nazuna pointed her chin at the changing room.

Ichi leaped out of the bath and raced to the changing room as Kogin and Kikumaru watched in amazement. When she opened the door, she saw a roomful of naked girls with their backs turned to each other, getting dressed or holding something modestly in front of themselves with one hand while they toweled dry. She couldn't see anyone's face.

"Haruna, are you here? The girl from Iojima?"

As Ichi scanned the room, over by the entrance a slim girl just starting to get dressed froze in place. When her eyes met Ichi's, she trembled.

"Why, you're Aiya Tama!"

Hearing her name called, the girl dropped her clothes and hugged Ichi. "I can't believe it!"

They clasped each other, naked, and wept. Ichi held Tama's arm tight and rubbed it over and over. That this arm belonging to Tama from her island was right here, right now, felt like a dream.

"What made you come?"

"My ma got sick."

"Oh no. That's awful. So sorry."

It felt good to talk in native dialect. No one else could understand what they said. Tama's mother and hers dove together. Tama's family lived on the eastern edge of the island, away from hers, but she and Tama had known each other growing up. They had both danced in festivals to celebrate good catches, among other things.

"Any news from the island?"

"Old man Kaibukuro died."

"Oh my!" Ichi gasped. Tama's arm felt firm and cool, even though she had just left the hot, steamy bath.

"Torite Hina married Sabatsu Matsuzo."

"Oh my!"

Hina was a strong-minded girl, Matsuzo a skilled fisherman.

"And Inamura Shokkichi took a wife."

Ichi was silent. She let go of Tama's arm. A wife? He'd come here selling cows in mid-April and stayed the night. That was nearly six months ago and, come to think of it, he hadn't shown his face since.

"Shokkichi's married?"

"Yep. To the daughter of a big farmer in Satsuma. A real beauty."

Ichi trembled. "When was this?" Her voice was unsteady.

"March of this year, I think. The cherry blossoms were out."

Then he was married when he came. When they slept together and he praised her skill in bed, he'd had a wife waiting for him at home on the island.

Shokkichi, you liar!

Tama bent over and picked up her patched and shabby clothes off the floor, where she had dropped them. While she dressed, Ichi dried herself with a towel. She had no desire to go back in and finish her bath.

Before long the new girls started coming to the Female Industrial School. They came not of their own volition but because their employers required it. They had to learn to read and write various names: their own, first of all, as well as the name of the place where they worked, the names of the proprietor and proprietress, and the names of clients and colleagues. They needed arithmetic to keep track of their earnings. They needed to learn to write clients' addresses, too, and practice writing letters to their clients.

The new girls would wear red kimonos with flowing sleeves and go on display with the others behind the wooden lattice facing the street. Ichi was young and small for her age, so although she had been at the Shinonome for eighteen months now, she still wore a red kimono and would continue to do so until the coming winter.

The familiar classroom now held nearly forty students in a dozen rows, three to a desk. Ichi and her group had finally advanced to the cherry-blossom class. Tetsuko was still their teacher; the new peach-blossom class met on odd-numbered days, the cherry-blossom class on even-numbered days.

"Good afternoon, teacher!"

One odd-numbered day, the classroom buzzed as everyone called out the usual greeting at the beginning of class. Tetsuko saw Ichi sitting in the very back. She came every day, studying in both classes. The desk where she now sat was a bit crowded, with four girls squeezed in.

Tetsuko's introductory lesson was always the same. Her kimono sleeves tied neatly out of the way, she picked up a piece of chalk and wrote on the blackboard the characters for "sun," just as she had done eighteen months before.

"Today we will learn to write the names for things around us. These characters represent the sun. Why learn to write these characters before any others? Because nothing and no one in the world is more important than the sun."

The new girls listened in silence.

"Do you know why?"

No response.

Tetsuko wasn't surprised that girls who had come here from the countryside after being sold by their parents in the fall of 1904 should be incapable of answering the question. Completely illiterate, they couldn't write even their own names. They didn't know that the earth was round, or that it orbited the sun, or that life on earth depended on sunlight. They had never been taught anything of the world beyond their kitchens at home. Now they would devote their lives to learning about and finally coming to know one thing: men.

"You need to know about the sun. It enables us to live in good health. The sun is of supreme importance to us."

Silence. The girls looked blank.

"The emperor's important, too," Ichi said from the back row, craning her neck.

"Yes, he is. The emperor is important. Who else?" She looked around the classroom.

"Fathers," said a girl in the front row.

"Teachers," said her desk mate. "Teachers are important, right?"

"What about Saint Kobo Daishi?" asked someone else. "My grandma says he's really important."

Tetsuko nodded at each of these suggestions. Then she swept the room with her gaze. "But the sun is still more important."

This provoked a murmur.

"Without the sun, we could not go on living. It would certainly be terrible if anything happened to the emperor, but his death would not cause people or animals or trees or grass to die. And even without parents or teachers, we can survive."

"What about Saint Kobo Daishi?" someone said, and the room laughed.

"Well, what about him?" Tetsuko put her head on one side, contemplating. "It might be terrible if he disappeared from the next world, but in this world, we can get along without him."

Comparing what came first in the world of science with what came first in the worlds of politics or ethics or Buddhism was impossible. But people were living things, and they needed to understand what came first in the scientific world. If they set that aside and put the emperor or their father or Kobo Daishi first, the end result would be catastrophe, Tetsuko believed.

When she was young, the shogun, not the emperor, had come first. But the shogun had abandoned his retainers and surrendered to the emperor, and many of those he abandoned had gone on to lose their lives in battle.

These girls had been sold into prostitution in the name of filial piety, to serve their parents. The sun would never sell anyone, but all too often people were sold or killed because of the emperor or their parents or a deity.

The sun asked nothing of humans. All it did was pour on them the blessing of its light.

If the girls knew that the sun was the most important thing to them, they would be all right, Tetsuko thought. She proceeded to write more kanji characters on the blackboard—"moon," "star," "cloud"—and had the class write down the words and their readings.

"These are the sun's companions," she said.

The place where all these things existed was the world. She added the kanji for "sea," "land," "mountain," and "river." The girls had crossed sea and mountains and rivers to come to this small, artificial quarter.

She took the chalk and wrote two more words in kanji: "human" and "beast." Humans and beasts were differentiated by the presence or absence of fur. That and whether they could utter words and communicate using language. No more needed to be said, Tetsuko thought. After reading Fukuzawa Yukichi's *New Greater Learning for Women*, she was even less sure whether humans were superior to animals or if it was the other way around.

Next she wrote "man," "woman," "old person," "young person," and "child." Humans included men and women, the old and the young. Men and women mingled here in the pleasure quarter, buying and selling the pleasure of sexual love.

Tetsuko told the girls to copy all the words on the blackboard into their notebooks. The character for "beast" was difficult, sixteen strokes, but they needed to know it, too. You couldn't write about all the things in the world using only simple characters.

When Tetsuko used to work in the Yoshiwara pleasure quarter, her older friend Takeko, whose father was also a low-ranking samurai, once wrote this in her diary at night:

I will surely, surely flee this prison of bestial desire. I will escape from this cage of dirty, lecherous beasts. From now on I will live to fulfill this vow.

Reading those lines, Tetsuko had properly learned the character for "beast" for the first time. Her friend had splendidly achieved her goal and now lived in Berlin with her scholarly husband. Tetsuko herself had only half escaped the cage. She made a living teaching writing to women trapped in the prison of bestial desire.

Ichi stood up in the back of the room. Her finished paper dangled from her fingertips. She came to the front of the classroom and handed it to Tetsuko.

"Finished? Are you leaving now?"

"Yes'm. Goodbye."

Ichi slid the door open and went out.

The page of her journal lay on Tetsuko's desk.

September 21 Sunny Aoi Ichi

These days wherever I look
there are always more girls.
The place where I work is full of
girls girls girls nothing but girls.
Walking outside, I see girls girls nothing but
  girls.
The bath too has girls girls nothing but girls.

There are so many girls that men are all
    arrogant.
Girls go home!
Girls go back where you came from!
Bring lots of men instead!

Tetsuko looked up.

Ichi was out of sorts today.

Autumn had arrived, but the days were still warm. The large building was cool even in midsummer on the first floor, where the rooms for entertaining clients were, but the third floor, where the prostitutes lived, was steamy. The fourth floor, where the storage space and linen room were, was so hot that even in mid-September, anyone who went in would soon break out in a sweat.

Day after day, low-ranking prostitutes and newcomers gathered in the upper room they called "the inferno" for training sessions with old Otoku. The number of participants had increased so much that Otoku took out the partition between two large eight-mat rooms and spread out a thick red futon in the middle.

"Go down and get one of the manservants. Anyone will do." She pointed downstairs with the long bamboo ruler she used to rap the prostitutes on their behinds.

One of the girls nodded, flew downstairs, and brought back Yasuzo, who had been sweeping the road in front of the building. The usual victim was Hisakichi, a young man; Yasuzo was a heavyset man in his forties, none too pleased to be chosen, judging by his expression. When Otoku saw him, she was momentarily disconcerted: he had too much vigor.

The girls sat on the floor, tense with foreboding, while Yasuzo sat cross-legged in the middle of the futon, apparently resigned to his fate. The sight of him sitting there only increased their fear. Otoku scanned the room, and her eyes alighted on Otome, the girl in Shinonome's charge whom she hoped to develop into a top earner.

"You're Otome, aren't you? Take off your kimono and come over here in just your underkimono and underskirt."

The blood drained from Otome's face.

"Hurry and get undressed, will you!"

Otome stood and slipped off her kimono. Otoku tossed her a set of scarlet undergarments. "Good. When you've changed into these, go over to the futon and lie down."

Otome obediently picked her way between the other girls. Ichi's heart beat fast in sympathy as she remembered how she had felt that time she'd lain down with Hisakichi in front of everyone. She watched Otome step barefoot onto the vivid scarlet futon. The silk would feel cool against the soles of her feet.

Yasuzo regarded her with compassion.

"Yasuzo, you lie down. The customer should be stretched out comfortably on his back."

He did as told. His face and his open chest glistened with sweat. Otoku's forehead and strands of hair, too, dripped with perspiration as she issued instructions, crouched over the futon. The room was hot and close. The heat from so many bodies crowded together added to the oppressiveness.

Otome started to recline alongside Yasuzo.

"Tantalize him. Pull up your skirt just a little. Take your time and slide one leg in, then slowly let your toes show, so he sees them."

The flow of her movements was interrupted by these detailed instructions, and Otome seemed confused. When she had finished arranging herself on Yasuzo's left, Otoku's ruler whizzed through the air and struck her on the hip.

"Imbecile! What kind of a prostitute lies face up like a doll? This isn't your wedding night!" Otoku reached out and roughly forced her to turn facing Yasuzo, who lay motionless and stiff.

Ichi felt such tightness in her chest that she could hardly breathe. When her turn had come, she had gotten through it somehow. Never in her life had she suffered as much as then. Her vision had gone cloudy, her eyes seeming to shoot sparks as something inside her burned and charred. Yet watching Otome now was even more painful. She squirmed in discomfort, seeing herself on display.

"Otome, lower your right shoulder. Now put your right arm under Yasuzo's neck, while with your left hand you slowly caress him, from his chest to his belly and on down between his legs."

The silence was intense. The girls leaned forward, holding their breath as they watched. They were drenched in perspiration. Sweat soaked the collars of their kimonos and rolled down their backs, under their arms, between their breasts, and down their bellies. The room grew more and more humid. There was only the rustle of kimonos and Otome's painful breathing. Yasuzo made not a sound.

"Aaagh, I hate this!" Otome let out a long agonized cry. "I hate, hate, hate it!"

Otoku stood up, ruler in hand.

Yasuzo sat up on the futon, but Otome was faster. She jumped to her feet, shuddering. The front of her red underkimono was wide open, but she paid no attention as she elbowed her way through the crowd of girls and out the door. Her footsteps resounded as she charged down the stairs to the second floor, then the first.

Otoku followed stealthily behind, slinking like a tiger going after its prey.

The girls left behind held their breath and listened

for signs of what was transpiring below, while Yasuzo silently put himself to rights. Otoku was shouting to the servants to bring Otome to her. Otome shrieked in protest. Apparently someone had grabbed her and was holding her down. Then for a long time her far-away screams continued as she received her punishment. Her voice was high and shrill at first; then the sounds seemed inhuman; then they trailed off and disappeared.

The new girls at the Yoshidaya, Nazuna and Haruna, stopped coming to school. They missed two days in a row, then three. Most likely their mistress was keeping them away, said Kikumaru and Umekichi.

Ichi decided to pay a visit to the Yoshidaya after school. She took along a rice-flour confection, a treat unavailable on Iojima, to give to Haruna. Shinonome had received several from an admirer and had shared them with her.

The alleyway just off the main avenue had a clinging damp smell. She came to the Yoshidaya with its peeling signboard and humble red lattice on the second floor. It was still early, before the lamp-lighting, so no one was about. From just within came the voice of a young girl. Ichi darted around the corner, out of sight.

"I'll miss you so much. When does the boat leave?"

It was the voice of Tama, that is, Haruna, the girl she had just run into in the bath two days ago.

"Tomorrow morning. I'll come again," said a languid male voice.

A young man appeared. His face was turned away, so Ichi couldn't see his features, but she could clearly hear his voice in the narrow lane. There was no mistaking the owner of that voice she knew so well. It was Shokkichi from Iojima.

They had come on the same boat, she realized numbly. With boat service on the remote island limited, they had all traveled here together: Shokkichi to sell cows, Haruna to be sold, and the herd of cows. No doubt Shokkichi had slept with Haruna the past few nights. Her very first customer.

Shokkichi, you rat!

Ichi backed away, then ran back to the Shinonome. In her room, she found her new roommate, Otome, lying down as Tamagiku cooled her flushed and swollen face. Otome was lucky old Otoku had administered the beating. If a man had taken his fists to her, she'd be in far worse shape.

Ichi took out the confection from her sleeve and laid it by Otome's pillow. "Try this. It's strange . . . who'd have thought there was anything so tasty here in hell?" She gave a twisted smile.

That evening, after the lanterns were lit and the shamisen started up its nightly jangling, clients attracted by the lively atmosphere began to trickle in. The girls took their places behind the wooden lattice, lined up on display. Ichi and the other low-ranking prostitutes, including the newcomers, sat toward the rear.

Someone reached inside the lattice and laid a hand on Ichi's knee. "Hey, where are you lookin'? It's me!"

Ichi came to herself and recognized Shokkichi, standing there with a grin on his face.

"Oh? And who're you?"

"Don't be an idiot. I'm the only one for you, Mr. Shokkichi of Iojima!"

Ichi studied him. His nostrils were flared, his face beaming. *Moron*, she murmured under her breath.

"What do you want?"

"What do you think? I'm here to sleep with you! Come on," he added, and went around to the entrance.

Ichi remained where she was until Shokkichi came trotting back and urged her to hurry. She stood up.

Wearily, her skirt trailing sloppily, she went to the room where Shokkichi was waiting. Instead of jumping on her as he usually did, he seemed in no rush. He had only just come from the Yoshidaya, after all. He sat quietly drinking *shochu* spirits. Without a word, Ichi filled his cup, and he gulped the strong liquor down. People in southern Kyushu were big drinkers, and what they drank was shochu.

"You have some, too." He took the bottle and poured a cupful for Ichi. "Tonight I wanna talk."

Well, this was certainly out of character.

"Talk about what?"

"Something interesting. You'll see." He gulped down his drink.

"Go on then," she said listlessly.

"My cows can swim. You've gotta see it to believe it."

"Wow. You really are some liar." Ichi sighed.

"It's no lie! My cows can swim, I tell you. Once when the boat started to sink, seawater began seeping in, and damned if they didn't start paddling. Cow-paddling. They just paddled away like it was the most natural thing in the world."

Those enormous animals could float easily in the ocean, Shokkichi said. If you took them to the beach now and then and put them in the water, most cows would immediately start to move their legs back and forth, swimming with apparent ease.

"They half close their eyes and flare their nostrils. You can tell they like it."

"Huh." Ichi lay on the futon, listening. Soon nothing seemed to matter anymore. Her eyelids were heavy.

Sitting by the pillow, Shokkichi kept pouring his own drinks and talking.

"If I go back to the island and marry you, can I see the cows swim?" Ichi murmured sleepily.

"You bet. I'll show you." Shokkichi nodded.

What a liar.

"Thanks."

Ichi tried slowly to raise her drooping eyelids.

She was too sleepy. Too comfortable. She stretched out her arms and legs and dozed, grateful that for once she could just drift off to sleep. She would scold Shokkichi some other time. As she dozed, her head filled with a vision of the sea surrounding her island.

Cows' legs paddled in the water.

Slowly, slowly, the four-legged beasts paddled through the water in her dream.

No Parents for Prostitutes

One afternoon, Ichi ran downstairs as usual and was about to set off for school when she heard Tose calling her from the front office. Ichi braced herself for a scolding—but what had she done? Tose signaled for her to come in. She entered the room fearfully and sat down across from the proprietress.

"Your father is coming here tomorrow."

Ichi looked at her blankly. "What for?"

"I don't know. To see you, probably. The boat gets in tonight, so he should be here in the morning. Stay home from school tomorrow and wait for him."

Ichi's tense muscles relaxed. She wasn't being scolded after all; Tose was being kind to her.

Tose held a letter in her hands. The writing was cramped and uneven. Ichi had never seen her father's handwriting before, but she recognized it intuitively. On shore, he was always repairing his nets, examining them with thick fingers and flattened fingertips, and dexterously mending any tears. The nets in his care were beautiful when you held them up in the sunlight, but his writing was ill-formed and ugly, like smudged inkblots. Ichi's face grew hot.

"Okay, then I'm off!" She ran all the way to school, filled with happiness and inexplicable sadness.

Her classmates in the cherry-blossom class worked silently, copying difficult terms from the blackboard. The content of the lessons was becoming steadily more advanced.

Ichi took a seat in the back of the room next to Umeyakko, a slightly older prostitute who was like a big sister to the younger ones. Umeyakko worked at the Matsunoya, kitty-corner from the Shinonome.

"Just looking at the blackboard makes my head hurt," Umeyakko murmured, turning toward Ichi. "But you've gotta know your characters to survive. Otherwise it's work, work, work, and never a penny richer."

On the paper in front of her, Umeyakko had written "account book" and "debt carried over from the preceding month" in a fine, practiced hand. Ichi only recognized the shapes of the characters. Some were written on the cover of the book Tose showed her in the office every month, but as she couldn't read them, the cover might as well have been blank. Tose would open the book to that month's page and go on and on about it, but Ichi couldn't really follow.

Tetsuko explained that the numbers in the account book showed earnings for the month minus debt carried over from the month before. Monthly expenses were deducted as well, with the cost of food, lodging, oil, charcoal, medicine, clothing, face powder, and rouge all laid out in detail. Learning to read and write the characters for these everyday necessities was essential. Her gaze fell on Ichi. "Aoi Ichi, look at the blackboard and copy everything there."

Startled, Ichi ducked her head. She wanted to write her journal entry, but the look on Tetsuko's face told her not to try.

"There are less than two months left this year. Each of you needs to know the truth about the money you have earned putting your body and your health on the line. Has your debt from the previous month been properly reduced by your earnings? Or if the debt increased, is that really true? Learn to read and understand what is written in your account book. Otherwise . . ."

Tetsuko hesitated.

Sometimes a brothel's one-sided bookkeeping meant that rather than decrease over time, debts ballooned. The accounts of illiterate prostitutes were fudged, and when a woman's contract ended with her debt unsettled, she was kept on for the rest of her life as a menial, never free.

Checking the blackboard with bleary eyes, Ichi

copied a series of characters so complicated, they looked to her like tangles of black nails: "prostitute's fee," "owner's revenue," "prostitute's revenue," "monthly installment," "added debt."

The prostitute's fee was the money each of them earned by working. Of that amount, the owner took approximately half; that was his revenue. Further deductions were made for food, living expenses, and miscellaneous expenses. Dishonest establishments charged exorbitant prices for inferior meals and registered purchases of nonexistent kimonos, fiddling with the books so that prostitutes' finances were always in the red. Each month's additional debt was added to the accrued total. However much they wore themselves out working, they could never get ahead.

The cost of meals was not a great problem, since everyone ate the same food, but even a less expensive kimono cost at least eight yen, the starting monthly salary of a primary school teacher or a policeman. But a prostitute had to have plenty of kimonos; she couldn't attract clients wearing a soiled one. On average, a prostitute's revenue ranged from ten to fifteen yen a month, hardly enough to cover the cost of her wardrobe. Payment was made in monthly installments.

"Class, listen. You must all learn to read and write the characters for personal belongings. This may seem like a great deal of trouble now, but in the end it is well worth it." They needed to pay attention to miscellaneous expenses recorded in their account books, verifying that the costs of individual items matched the total.

"Copy these down, please." Tetsuko wrote out the kanji for a series of familiar words, along with the pronunciations in kana: "kimono," "underkimono," "underskirt," "tabi," "face powder," "rouge," "soap," "tobacco," "medicine fee," "doctor's fee," "oil fee," "charcoal fee," "bath fee."

"Where I work," muttered Umeyakko, "you have to watch out or they'll charge you for coal in the summertime." Sometimes they charged for lamp oil even on nights when she had no clients and her lamps went unlit.

Tetsuko tapped the blackboard. "Attention, please. The category you have to watch the most carefully is 'added debt.' This is tacked on to your existing debt, so you need to check to make sure the numbers are right. To do that, you have to know the special characters that are used in transcribing sums of money."

She proceeded to write out kanji for the numerals from 1 to 10, using alternative, more difficult characters for 1, 2, 3, and 10. Then she had the students practice writing their ages, using the new characters where appropriate.

"Aoi Ichi, come up here and write your age."

After studying what Tetsuko had written, Ichi

scrawled "16" correctly. She returned to her seat, and Tetsuko called next on Matsuyama Setsu, or Hanaji, to write her age. Hanaji wrote "21" on the board but got it wrong, using an incorrect mix of kanji.

"Not quite," said Tetsuko. "Can anyone show us how this ought to be written?"

Kogin stood up and smoothly wrote out the correct answer on the blackboard.

"That is exactly right. The numbers 1, 2, and 3 are written using difficult characters on purpose, to prevent anyone from coming along afterward and altering what is written. These are the numerals used in calculating your debt, so it is vital that you get to know them."

Today's lesson was challenging.

"Now suppose we add Aoi Ichi's age and Matsuyama Setsu's age together. How many is that? Write the answer on your paper."

"Whaaat?" said Umeyakko aloud. The class giggled. "Ma'am, that's impossible. I haven't got enough fingers to count that high."

"Then borrow your desk mate's fingers. Anyone who cannot do arithmetic will find it next to impossible to fulfill her contract and leave the licensed quarter. Believe me, calculating the money you owe is the same as calculating your very life. Use your fingers and your toes if you have to, and count for all you are worth."

Umeyakko counted over and over on her fingers, raising and lowering them, before writing "37" on her paper.

"Count me out!" Ichi muttered under her breath. She bent her head over the paper on her desk and wrote her thoughts, as usual.

November 10 Light rain in the morning
Aoi Ichi
Tomorrow my pa is coming from Iojima.
Coming from far across the ocean to see me.
When he sees me what face will he make?
Its all I think about.
I wont be able to sleep tonight.
There are lots of men
but only one I love—
my one and only pa.

On the way back from school, Ichi walked partway with Hanaji and Umeyakko. "I'm going to stop at Hanakawa, so go on without me." She sounded excited. Hanakawa was a small store that sold notions and novelties.

"Can I come too?" asked Hanaji. "What are you going to buy, Kojika?"

"My pa's coming here tomorrow! I'm buying presents for him to take to my mother and my big sister."

"Really? My pa's coming the day after tomorrow. I'll buy some presents, too!"

Working had its advantages. The two of them, aged sixteen and twenty-one, could afford gifts for their families back home. Normally they had nothing to spend their money on, but now they could put it to good use. Ichi wanted to get a mirror and comb for her sister, and for her mother tabi socks for the New Year. They were just about to run off to the store when they heard Umeyakko's voice behind them, sounding puzzled: "Wait. You both got a letter from your pa?"

"Not me," said Hanaji. "I heard about it from the mistress."

"So did I!" Ichi said.

Hanaji had an odd look on her face. "Are you saying my pa won't come?"

"No, never mind, it's nothing," Umeyakko stammered. "I hope you see him." She left them in front of Hanakawa.

That night, Ichi missed out on a client. To "miss out" was to fail to get something. You could miss out on a meal, work, a lover, or just about anything. The verb had a wide application in the quarter.

Alone in her room, Ichi sat at her desk doing writing exercises while Tamagiku was out assisting the oiran at a banquet. Working was no fun, but knowing that tonight no one had wanted her made Ichi feel cut off from the world.

Tetsuko was right. A prostitute lived to pay off her debt. Earning money meant earning life, and tonight Ichi had missed out on the opportunity to do so.

She practiced writing the characters they had been taught at school that day, and then for good measure she wrote down her Hanakawa purchases: two pairs of women's tabi, sixteen sen. One hand mirror, twelve sen. One comb, seven sen. To calculate the total, she spread out her hands and counted on her fingers: sixteen and twelve made twenty-eight, plus seven . . . thirty-five sen in all.

Yesterday Tose had shown Ichi her earnings for the previous month: seventeen yen. In other words, she had earned just under seventy sen per day. So on top of missing out on work, she had spent half a day's earnings on gifts.

Tamagiku was taking a long time getting back.

Ichi laid out the tabi, the hand mirror, and the comb by her futon and went to sleep.

That night she dreamed that her father stepped nervously inside the Shinonome. She called out "Pa!" and ran to him, her heart singing.

In the morning, Ichi swept the street in front of the building. Takezo came out with a bamboo broom, but she chased him away. "I'll do it!"

When her colleagues trooped out on their way to the bathhouse, she went right on sweeping. "I'm not going today!"

In a while, they all came back and set off for school. Even then, Ichi did not budge from the entrance. After a while Takezo poked his head out and looked at her, and then Tose came out.

"Kojika."

Ichi turned her head.

"Your pa's not coming till later, Kojika. A messenger came from the harbor inn where he's staying." Tose's voice was gentle.

"He's not coming till later?"

"That's right. So go ahead and run off to school. I'll have him wait for you." Tose took the broom from Ichi's hand.

"Well then, I might as well go." Ichi hurried upstairs to get her writing things. If she ran, she could still catch up with the others. School was the one place where she felt free to be herself. Soon she flew out the door carrying a cloth bundle.

After Ichi was gone, Tose looked around. "Yoo-hoo, Mr. Aoi Seizo? You can come out now."

From the shadows emerged a man with a tanned and leathery face. He was poorly dressed and empty-handed. Afraid to look his daughter in the eye, he had been hiding since early that morning. Tose beckoned to him to come inside. He was built like a bonito, thin but strong from his life as a fisherman. He had come to pile another layer of debt on the shoulders of his sixteen-year-old daughter.

Inside the office, someone served green tea, and Saito brought out the ledger. As they prepared to draw up a new promissory note, Saito offered Ichi's father an inkstone and brush, but he waved them away. He asked someone else to write it. He could read, he said.

Tose picked up the brush and smoothly wrote the following:

> Promissory Note
>
> I, Aoi Seizo, acknowledge that on this day, November 11, 1904, I received from Hajima Mohei the sum of 150 yen, which will be added to the existing debt of 330 yen for a total of 480 yen. I hereby consent to this arrangement.
>
> Aoi Seizo
> Father of Ichi
> Seto, Oshima-gun, Iojima,
> Kagoshima Prefecture

Saito read the document aloud.

Sitting with his legs folded under him on the tatami floor, his hands tightly grasping his knees, Seizo nodded.

This was a certificate of added debt, one of the terms

Tetsuko had written on the blackboard. The Shinonome was the preeminent brothel in the quarter, and its financial records were on the level. However, any number of such certificates could be issued without prior notification. A child was the parents' possession and could be freely bought and sold. A parent's consent was all it took to make the increased obligation official.

Impoverished farmers and fishermen across the country, hard pressed toward the end of the year, used their daughters' flesh to supplement the family income. Some talked it over candidly with their daughters, but others, like Seizo, borrowed the extra money furtively and fled. The Shinonome management did not look kindly on the second type of parent, for then they were left with the painful task of showing the girl the promissory note and making her understand.

After Seizo had slunk off, Ichi returned from school, walking in big strides like a man, little suspecting what had happened behind her back.

"My pa here yet?" she called loudly to Saito. He stiffened. "Ain't he here yet, Saito? C'mon!" She kicked off her wooden geta in the entrance.

Saito stared silently at the ledger, his lips pressed tightly together in annoyance.

After her father left, Ichi spent several days staring vacantly out of the window. Even when her name was called, she remained in a trance. When she poured sake for a client at a banquet, she spilled it. When she slept with a customer, she lay unmoving like a doll. Sometimes the customer grew irate and Tose had to step in to smooth things over.

Shinonome had had enough. After her bath one morning, she lay on her silk futon and had Ichi rub her back. "Now that you have added debt, this is no time to be slacking off. You'll only make things worse for yourself. This moment is crucial. Think carefully and show good sense."

The added debt meant that she must work that much harder to win clients' favor and devotion so that they would keep on asking for her.

"Don't talk to me about good sense!" Ichi shot back. She trembled, near tears. Her father was the one lacking sense. How dare Shinonome lecture her about being sensible!

"You are quite right." The oiran acquiesced with a slight nod.

"I did some calculating about my debt."

"You did? How?"

Ichi left off massaging Shinonome and from the front of her kimono took out a folded paper chockablock with messy figures.

The added debt had brought Ichi's total to 480 yen. Her earnings the previous month came to seventeen yen, putting her in the middle of the bottom third of all the house prostitutes. This was reasonable, considering her age. Half of her earnings went to Mohei, and after deductions for clothes, food, and miscellaneous expenses, five yen, seventy sen, remained. That was Ichi's revenue, her net income for the month.

"I calculated how many years it'd take to pay off 480 yen at the rate of five yen a month."

All her fingers and all her toes hadn't been enough to do the calculation. There were twelve months in a year, so on a sheet of paper she'd written the kanji for "5" twelve times and discovered that in one year she could pay back sixty yen. Then she'd written "60" eight times, which added up to 480, and she had understood that her debt would be paid off in eight years.

"I checked it over and over."

The result was always the same: eight years. But by that calculation, she would have next to nothing left to spend on herself. Realistically, the amount she could pay back each month would be less than five yen.

"And there are sure to be times when I get sick and can't work."

Staying healthy for eight years and taking clients every day without stopping was key. To do that, she would need a demon's strength and hardness of heart. As she told Shinonome this, Ichi dug into the oiran's back with her short fingers. Shinonome endured the pain with a grimace.

"If I'm not careful, my contract'll expire before I've paid off my debt." Then she would have two options: either stay on as cook or transfer to one of the cheaper establishments known as hells.

All along, Ichi had assumed that one day she could return to her island and swim again with the giant sea turtles. Now she knew that from the day she left home, that had been an impossible dream.

"Your earnings rise over time, you know," Shinonome reminded her, lying on her stomach. "If you become popular, you can make ten or twenty yen a day and pay off your debt that much faster."

"Only if you're beautiful," Ichi murmured. She was all too aware of her snub nose. Some of her colleagues were good-looking, but even they wore themselves out working. Plain girls had it worse.

We're not oirans! It's different for us!

Ichi's colleagues whispered that Shinonome earned two hundred yen each time she slept with a client. A second night made it four hundred yen; a third, and she had earned enough to wipe out Ichi's eight-year debt and live in leisure for a year or two besides.

Of course, an oiran's two hundred yen paid for everything from her own splendid kimonos, sashes, over-robes, and hair baubles to the wardrobes of any girls under her wing, like Tamagiku and Ichi, as well as the bills of hairdressers, doctors, and other specialists. An oiran truly nurtured everyone around her.

Money, money, money: people throughout the pleasure district were equally tormented.

"Even if my earnings go up, Pa'll be back."

The realization struck Ichi like a bolt of lightning. Her pa was bound to return. The year after selling her, he had already come to borrow more. Whether he had used the first round of money to buy a new fishing boat or repair the old one, she didn't know, but she knew the 150 yen he'd received this time wouldn't last, either.

In poor households there was a deep hole that swallowed money. Sickness, injury, bad harvests, poor catches: the hole was bottomless. Try as they might, the family members never could fill it. Ichi had known this since she was a child.

"Oh, that feels so much better." Shinonome sat up, stretching her neck. Even an oiran, whose body was made of money, had burdens that weighed her down. "Thank you. Take this and have something nice to eat with your friends." She slipped ten sen into Ichi's palm. "I heard what you said today. I won't forget it. Now you must stop moping around and being out of temper at work."

"Yes'm." Ichi nodded and left Shinonome's apartment.

She ran into Hanaji at the top of the stairs. Hanaji

looked up in surprise as they nearly collided, her face a stony white. Ichi was shocked. She hadn't seen Hanaji since the day Ichi's pa came.

Perhaps Hanaji hadn't been able to see her pa, either.

"Are you going to school?" Ichi asked, standing on the narrow stairway. Hanaji was carrying her writing box, wrapped in cloth.

"I'm going to say goodbye to the teacher," Hanaji said quietly.

Ichi was mystified. "Goodbye?"

"I'm going to Shikoku. My pa resold me to some pleasure district in Marugame on Shikoku."

"He resold you?"

"Yeah. He used the money from there to pay off the debt here. Then he borrowed even more."

Ichi pursed her lips. This was no place to be having this discussion. "Let's go outside."

Having Kogin and Kikumaru join them right now would be awkward, so they hurried out. Ichi remembered that on the way back from school the other day, Umeyakko of the Matsunoya had said something odd. She and Hanaji had been happy and excited, little knowing that a father who traveled from afar to the brothel where his daughter worked did so for one reason only.

"November back home is when lots of girls get sold," Hanaji seemed to be reminiscing. Families sold their daughters because otherwise the following year would never come. They were desperate.

"When will you go to Shikoku?"

"The day after tomorrow. A man who buys women is coming to take me. I'll get on the boat and off I'll go."

Ichi had never even heard of Marugame.

"There's no better place to work than the Shinonome," Hanaji said. "The owner's rich and he treats us fair and square."

Hanaji and Ichi walked along with their heads hanging, their eyes on their feet.

They arrived at school early. Tetsuko was out in front of the cherry-blossom classroom, sweeping. Ichi tugged on her sleeve, and they went inside.

Hanaji untied her cloth bundle and took out a piece of paper, unfolded it, and handed it to Tetsuko. It seemed to be a copy of a promissory note, identical in form to the one Ichi had received. Hajima Mohei's solid writing attested to the immutable facts therein.

Tetsuko looked it over. "This is actually a receipt for a deposit paid by the brothel where you will be going." She explained that a portion of the money paid to the Fukuju brothel in Shikoku, where Hanaji had been resold, would go toward paying off her debt at the Shinonome. But as Hanaji had not yet officially transferred to the Fukuju, the figure written on the paper represented a deposit.

"Agh, it's so confusing!"

"Aoi Ichi, pay attention to financial matters, or someday you will be sorry."

"Someday" was already here. The night before, Ichi had cried herself to sleep.

"Matsuyama Setsu, the balance of your debt to the Shinonome is 320 yen. And I see your father decided to borrow an additional 250 yen from the Fukuju in Shikoku."

Hanaji stared into space.

Ichi bent her head and counted on her fingers. Unbelievable! Hanaji's body was now valued at 570 yen.

"Parents are the most terrifying thing in the world," Hanaji said. She looked at Tetsuko. "You tell us to respect our parents, but mine are eating me alive. They'll go on selling me and reselling me as long as they can. Running away from work won't do any good. I want to run away from my parents."

What Hanaji was saying seemed to Ichi to belong to some far-off world. When she imagined Hanaji's parents, the father had the head of a tiger, the mother the head of a monstrous cat. Ichi's parents were human. If she ever saw them again, she would fall weeping into their arms. She would go with them anywhere and never ever leave their side.

"Running away from your parents is the same as running away from your place of work. Matsuyama Setsu, you must not do anything rash. If you did succeed in running away, how would you live? A former prostitute has no way to get by in this world." Tetsuko tried to reason with Hanaji, who was in the grip of fierce emotions.

Out in the hallway, they heard the sound of voices and approaching footsteps. It was time for the cherry-blossom class to begin.

Hanaji hastily refolded the receipt and put it away. Tetsuko tied up the sleeves of her kimono with a cord.

The next morning, before anyone knew it, Hanaji was gone. She never came back to the Female Industrial School. To Ichi it felt like a bad dream.

Meanwhile, Tetsuko continued teaching new vocabulary and giving assignments involving the numerals used in financial documents. By mid-November, several more wretched men from afar had appeared in the quarter: two, three, then a fourth. They were fathers bent on devouring their daughters.

The ability to do financial calculations was more important to the class than the ability to write coaxing letters to clients, Tetsuko believed. Poor people needed education. They needed the advantages that education alone could provide.

One sentence by Fukuzawa Yukichi stuck in her mind. It was from an editorial in *Jiji Shimpo* entitled "Poverty and Riches, Intellect and Ignorance": "He who is most to be feared is a man who is poor and intelligent." Tetsuko agreed that a man with brains deserved respect, however poor he might be. When she read that sentence, she'd thought, *Yes! That's exactly right.* But as she read on, she found that Fukuzawa Yukichi and she didn't think the same way after all.

"The thinking of a man of intellect is lofty and grand, and his mind is constantly at work," he wrote. But poverty would make such a man suffer others' contempt and force him on occasion to curry favor, filling him with the distress of a "caged tiger"—a tiger so bursting with pent-up frustration and rage that there was no telling when it might explode and run wild.

> With no way to vent his frustrations, the penniless intellectual will perceive the workings of society as unjust and seek incessantly to go on the attack against them, calling for private property to be abolished or for all lands to be made public.

He would demand higher wages and shorter working hours; hence the workers' strikes now roiling the nation.

Tetsuko could hardly believe that these were the words of the same man who had boldly written, "Heaven does not create one person above or below another."

Yukichi further wrote, "It is necessary to consider

the advantages and disadvantages of giving an education to the poor."

Whom did he mean by "the poor"?

Though her father had been a samurai, Tetsuko's family had been poor, living on a meager stipend in a ramshackle house. Fukuzawa Yukichi was the son of a still more impoverished samurai in the Nakatsu domain of Kyushu. Had he not received an exceptional education thanks to the generosity of the domain lord and thereby risen to his present eminence, his great frustration vented? Tetsuko's blood boiled.

Here in the red-light district, she hoped that the prostitutes would become caged tigresses and explode one day soon by going on strike, though without the violence of the Nagasaki shipbuilders. Yes. Could that not happen?

She stood still in front of the blackboard, her hand frozen in midair.

One morning, a misty rain fell silently, like Hanaji's tears.

The cherry-blossom classroom was empty before class. On Tetsuko's desk lay a single sheet of paper that Ichi must have come and laid there unseen.

November 16 Rain Aoi Ichi
My pa came without a word
and left without a word.

Just like the wind.
As if he were formless.
If my pa is formless
why shouldnt I erase him?
Let my parents disappear!
The sky is vast
and swimming with clouds.
Having no parents
means nothing to me.

Ma'am, please use this hand mirror I bought for my big sister.

Ichi

On a corner of the paper lay a small mirror.

A Day Like New Year's Day

Yunami was the first to bring up how much the Shinonome charged for tobacco. "Anywhere else, the tobacco I smoke costs fifty sen for five ounces. Here it costs sixty-five sen! *Way* too much. Tobacco is a tool of the trade. They're not going to listen if I complain, but I mean to anyway. I just can't let it go."

Yunami and her colleagues were in the refectory having lunch. They were *tenjin*s, next in rank behind the oiran. Shinonome ate from a fine tray in the privacy of her room, with only her kamuro to wait on her. The highest-ranking courtesans in the refectory were the eight tenjins. They all nodded in agreement.

"I've always thought the very same thing," said the one named Shibagaki. "Anyone can go without food for a day, but to do our job we simply have to have tobacco. Letting ourselves run out of it would be the end!" She pointed a chopstick at her neck and turned it as if tightening a noose. A hush fell over the room. Now not only the other tenjins but everyone having lunch was listening.

A young girl like Ichi didn't smoke. As the prostitutes grew accustomed to the work, however, they relied on tobacco more and more.

At dusk when the shamisen began to play, a crowd of men gathered outside the lattice to look the women over and make their choices. But the prostitutes did not just sit quietly and wait to be chosen; they, too, passed judgment on potential customers. When one of them found a likely-looking candidate, she would light a long red lacquered pipe, take a slow drag on it, then offer it to him through the lattice. This was one of their seductive devices. If the man was so inclined, he would accept the pipe and head inside.

Ichi knew exactly how much Shinonome paid for tobacco, since she was frequently sent downstairs to buy the most expensive kind. If she could buy it elsewhere, she would save the oiran a great deal of money. But everyone was required to buy tobacco at the office, a month's supply at a time.

"Since it's a tool of our trade, they ought to mark it down for us," said Shibagaki.

Yunami tossed her chopsticks and bowl on the tray in disgust. "Ooh, it makes me so mad! Seven sen for a bowl of miso soup over rice with boiled greens on the side! If we ate anywhere else, for just three sen we'd get this and an egg besides. How are we supposed to build up our strength eating like crickets?"

The day before, Yunami had again quarreled with Saito. Everyone knew it. She was in a bad mood. She stood up and said, "I'm not working tonight!" Then she walked out of the room.

Everyone sucked in their breath. This was just like the shipbuilders' strike they had heard so much about.

November days were short. By the time Ichi came back from school, it was already dark out, and before long the strains of the shamisen announced that the Shinonome was open for business. Ichi went to Yunami's room on the third floor and looked inside.

Yunami was sitting with one knee raised, smoking, her red lacquered pipe sticking out of her mouth at an oblique angle.

A couple of Ichi's colleagues came along, and the three of them stood in a cluster at the door, watching to see what would happen.

"Move it, move it!" Shibagaki pushed them out of the way and charged into the room. "What's this? You're really going through with it?"

In the middle of the room, Yunami was writing on a piece of paper in a beautiful hand.

> Due to the extremely poor conditions at the Shinonome, I hereby declare that I will not work. I request that conditions be improved.
>
> Signed,
> Yunami
> November 20

The phrasing was familiar. It resembled the wording of the Nagasaki strike declaration they had read in the newspaper.

Yunami picked up the piece of paper, the ink still wet, and strode out into the hallway with a look of determination. Ichi and her colleagues jumped back, out of her way. She proceeded calmly down the stairs with Shibagaki right on her heels, followed in single file by Ichi, Kogin, and Umekichi, with Tamagiku bringing up the rear.

Yunami marched past the office. Hearing the commotion, Saito stuck his head out of the door. The tenjin proceeded to the refectory, where the others were still eating, and stopped at the wooden door.

"Bring me some grains of rice!" she ordered. A scullery maid named San lifted the lid of the rice kettle, scooped up a few grains of barley rice with her fingers, and gave them to Yunami to use as glue.

The paper fastened to the door reminded Ichi of New Year's, when white paper strips with writing on them hung from the god-shelf, the household Shinto altar. The whiteness of this paper seemed no less divine. It was a beautiful sight. A crowd quickly formed as the news spread.

Saito stomped over. Lacking authority to pull down the paper, he turned purple and yelled: "Th-the master and mistress are on their way! Yunami, you'll be sorry you ever did this!"

Shibagaki brushed the fuming manager aside and planted herself in front of the notice. She waved an ink-dipped brush from the office in front of Saito and then, in large, bold letters, added her name:

In solidarity
Shibagaki

Lowering her brush, she turned and looked around at the collection of women standing there regarding her in troubled silence. "You're pitiful," she said in a low voice. "With something like this, the more who join in, the stronger we are. If it's just one or two, we'll be crushed."

Ichi worried that Yunami and Shibagaki might suffer some dreadful punishment. Even if they were tenjins, there was no knowing what atrocities might take place behind the scenes. She pushed her way to the front and borrowed Shibagaki's brush. She didn't smoke, but someday she'd have to. Next to Shibagaki's name, she wrote "Kojika" in small letters.

Kogin took the brush from Ichi and added her name, too. Umekichi was next.

"If the new girls are signing up, I guess we'd better," said Harukoma, a leader among the senior prostitutes, and stepped boldly forward.

The refectory was suddenly filled with murmurs.

What did you do in a strike, anyway? All anyone knew was rumors about workers at the big shipyard across the harbor. But they had also heard that in the UK, a strike meant doing nothing at all, not lifting a finger to do your work. Should they join in with Yunami and the rest, or refrain in fear of Mohei's reprisals? The women wavered, torn. Only Ichi was unconcerned. She was used to beatings and scoldings, and her father had just increased her burden of debt. She had nothing more to fear. Let them do their worst!

Mohei and Tose had not yet shown themselves. The uncommitted prostitutes drifted nervously upstairs, leaving Yunami and her supporters below.

After a while the owners did appear, but the front office stayed eerily quiet, its silence unbroken by shouts from Mohei or screeches from Tose. At any moment the tempest would break, all felt sure, but time passed without incident. Ichi was mystified.

The situation remained unresolved at nighttime.

Shinonome took Tamagiku with her to entertain a client. On the way out, Tamagiku turned and glared at Ichi, as if to say, *Don't blame me when this ends badly for you.* What Shinonome was thinking was impossible to say; her lovely face was impassive.

From the top of the stairs, Ichi peered down at the entrance. The night was as lively as ever. Outside, except for the six on strike, the women sat behind the lattice with long red pipes at the ready, waiting for a customer of their liking to appear. The strains of the shamisen filled the air.

Ichi visited Kogin and Umekichi in their room. With nothing better to do, they were trimming their toenails.

"It's nice not to have to work at night for a change," said Umekichi.

"It's so quiet," said Kogin. The large room was deserted.

"Yeah," said Umekichi. "It's like all the people in the world just vanished."

"God swept them all away with his broom." Kogin giggled.

The clicking of toenail clippers reverberated in the silence. From next door came the low murmur of voices: Yunami, Shibagaki, and Harukoma, planning their next move, perhaps.

The quiet was too deep.

Ichi was strangely moved. All movement had ceased; a hush had settled over the world.

"Feels like New Year's." She brought out some candies she had tucked into her kimono, shared them, and slipped one into her mouth. Here, out of earshot of bawdy talk between men and women, the night was serene and pure, exactly as if tomorrow really would be the start of a new year.

The loud, boisterous gaiety of past nights seemed unreal. Then, women had danced and sung under brilliant lights while the shamisen resounded, drinks were poured, and couples engaged in light banter until finally they retired to the bedchamber and opened their legs to reveal the unsightly, poisonous flowers within.

Ichi pictured these things, feeling as if she were trapped in a weird dream from which tonight was a rare, brief respite.

When Ichi went down to breakfast in the morning, the notice was still up on the refectory door, undisturbed by Mohei. A new piece of paper was there, too, with a long list of names written in a variety of hands, some skilled and some unskilled, in characters large and small, some tilted and some squished.

Kazuki
Hanasode
Haruwaka

Yubune
Beniyakko
Mainosuke
Shiraume
Kikumaru
Tsurukichi
Tachibana
Yugiri
Sammaru
Tomoe
Toyowaka
Kuretake
Kikuya
Hanataro
Yukinosuke
Tamaki
Katsura
Miyoji

Ichi stood stock still, staring in wonder. Twenty-one people had joined the strike overnight. That made twenty-seven altogether. If Saito set out to slap all of them in the face, at least it would take time. His hand might even get swollen!

Mohei, Tose, and Saito must all be at their wits' end, she thought as she went to sit at her place. Her tray wasn't there. Seated next to her, Kaede, who was sipping miso soup as usual, explained: "They said no meals for anyone who signs the paper."

"But we pay for our food in advance."

"The cook has to prepare it." Kaede put her mouth close to Ichi's ear and whispered: "They said anyone who doesn't work here isn't one of us, and if outsiders want to eat the food, they'll have to pay for labor."

So Mohei had made a move.

Ichi looked around the room, noticing gaps here and there like missing teeth. Twenty-seven of the eighty would have to go without breakfast.

The refectory was by now nearly full. Those denied breakfast started to protest. Otoku walked around with a sneer on her face, holding a cracked bowl. "The cost of cooking breakfast is two sen. If you want to eat, put your money right here."

"Humph," scoffed Shibagaki. "If we went out to eat, for three sen we could have a hot bowl of udon with a nice piece of deep-fried tofu on top. Why pay two sen for a lousy bowl of barley rice?" She walked right past the old woman toward the back door.

Ichi followed. Shibagaki would find them somewhere to eat. Kogin and Umekichi came, too.

"Come on, everybody!" said Shibagaki. "Let's all have udon with an egg on it to build up our strength. The egg will be my treat." Tenjins were no less generous than oirans in looking out for their juniors. One after another, the udon eaters filed out, talking as they headed for the main avenue.

At this early hour, the street was still asleep, empty except for a few all-night clients on their way home. The udon shop stayed open to serve them. The parade of women at such an hour brought curious faces to upper-story windows along the way. A few early risers were walking toward the bathhouse, towel and soap in hand. Ichi and her companions had all the time in the world.

Shafts of morning sun fell on the rooftops, covering them in gleaming gold.

After downing a steaming bowl of udon with deep-fried tofu and an egg, Ichi went to the bathhouse and had a leisurely soak. She washed herself carefully, but since she hadn't had a customer the night before, she wasn't soiled to begin with. The hour was still early, the bath nearly empty.

"What'll we do after this?" Kogin sounded excited. Only her head was above the hot water.

"What if we go back to sleep?" whispered Umekichi.

Now that they weren't working, they could do whatever they wanted.

"I'm going to go to school and study." That was all Ichi wanted to do.

Ichi arrived at school very early. Tetsuko wasn't there yet. The old man who cleaned the ikebana and sewing rooms at the end of the hallway had just arrived and was unlocking the door. Ichi waited outside the cherry-blossom classroom and soon saw Tetsuko approaching.

Tetsuko was talking to someone as she walked. Her companion was a slender, graceful young woman wearing a radiant, rainbow-colored silk jacket over her kimono as protection against the winter wind. Lit by the morning sun, the young woman's face glowed with the beauty of Benten-sama, the goddess of wisdom and eloquence. As they came closer, Ichi saw that it was indeed Shinonome.

When Ichi left for school, Shinonome hadn't been in her room. "She went out," Tamagiku had said, sounding bored, sulking because she'd been left behind. Shinonome must have waited somewhere to intercept Tetsuko as she came from beyond the great gate on her way to work. What could the two of them be talking about?

Ichi ran up to them, calling out a cheery "Good morning!"

"Good morning, Aoi Ichi. Go ahead and open the door for us, if you please." Tetsuko handed Ichi a darkly gleaming key.

After unlocking the door to the classroom, Ichi drew water from the well and began cleaning the floor with a damp cloth. Sweeping with a broom would have required opening the windows, and that would make Shinonome cold.

Tetsuko thanked Ichi, put charcoal in the hibachi, and lit a fire. Then she led Shinonome to a desk by the window and sat down facing her.

Shinonome's brows were knit in a frown, and her mouth was tightly drawn. "So prostitutes' debts are really canceled? It sounds too good to be true. None of us has ever heard of such a thing." The oiran shook her head, laying her slim arms on the desktop. "Everyone knows that if they ran away, debt collectors would hound their parents without mercy. That fear makes them keep going despite their tears." She sounded very upset.

Tetsuko placed her hands in her lap and began to speak calmly. "Yes, a law called the Prostitute Liberation Law was issued back in 1872. But it was only a formality and never enforced. Debts were never canceled, and the right of prostitutes to regain their freedom was never recognized."

"I never knew anything about it."

"At the time, I believed it was true. I escaped and went to the police with a colleague. We sought protection, but we were marched back and received a terrible beating. That is when we realized that the police were on the side of the brothel owners."

"Why did the government pass such a hollow law?"

"Around that time a Peruvian ship entered Yokohama Harbor, and a large number of Chinese slaves jumped overboard and escaped. A lawyer for the Peruvian side argued that Japan could not condemn human trafficking since the buying and selling of prostitutes was legal here."

"Goodness. So the government rushed to issue an edict banning forced prostitution in name only?"

"Exactly."

"How amazing that they also came up with the idea of canceling debts, even as a formality. It's all the more maddening." Shinonome's bluish eyebrows furrowed.

"That was from something odd called the Livestock Emancipation Law."

"Livestock?"

"Yes," Tetsuko said quietly, "like horses and cows. A law to liberate livestock."

"Are you telling me," Shinonome spoke even more softly, "they used that word to refer to prostitutes?"

"Exactly."

"But why?"

"Because prostitutes are not human, they said."

"Not human?"

"Lower than humans."

Shinonome bit her lip and listened in silence as Tetsuko's voice continued like the steady dripping of rain.

"The law stated that prostitutes have lost their human rights and are therefore the same as livestock. Just as no one expects an animal to repay a debt, a prostitute must not be asked to repay what she owes, either. The logic is horrific, but if that law had been enforced, my friend and I would have been extremely happy. It never was. And so, unable to walk away or escape, she and I had to endure years of hard labor, saddled with debt."

Shinonome stared at her fists on the desk. Ichi put down her cleaning cloth and poked her head out from between the desks. Shinonome's head hung low.

Such a beautiful cow, Ichi thought, ducking back down. How could anyone so lovely be a cow? Perhaps she was a horse.

Shinonome's pride had been dashed. A cow's straw rope now encircled her muddy neck. The two women sat face-to-face without speaking.

Ichi left the room to boil water for tea. She was at home in the school and knew where everything was. She set two cups of tea on a tray and carried them to the classroom, only to find that Shinonome had gotten up to leave. The oiran thanked Ichi, drank the tea, and left, her steps unsteady.

Class would soon begin. Footsteps rang in the hallway. Tetsuko rose and fastened her sleeves with a cord, while Ichi took the teacups back and washed them before returning to take her seat.

Tetsuko stood in front of the blackboard, chalk in

hand, and wrote out a couple of sentences commonly used as greetings on New Year's cards. After learning to read and write financial terms, now they would prepare for the coming of the New Year, just over a month away.

> Please accept my best wishes at the joyous start of a new year.
>
> How peaceful it is to hear the nightingale sing at the start of the year!

"There are various formulaic expressions used at the beginning of a letter. Copy these down, paying careful attention to the formation of each character. Remember, poor handwriting can ruin a letter, however fine the expressions you use. Focus on writing attractively."

Tetsuko's voice sailed right over Ichi's head.

Ichi bent over her paper and scribbled with all her might.

> **November 28 Cloudy Aoi Ichi**
> Yesterday, Yunami, the rest of the tenjins, and I worked out demands for the strike.
>
> We all put our heads together and Shibagaki wrote everything down on a big sheet of paper.
>
> We demand
> —lower price for tobacco.

—dinner even on days with no clients.
—fish once every three days.
—an added egg on days with many clients.
—in winter, charcoal for the hibachi even on days with no clients.
—lower price for kimonos, which we have to have for our job.
—two weeks leave after an abortion.
—no diseased clients.

The tenjins say theres lots more besides.
Think of other grievances, they say.
But my parents taught me never to complain.
Thinking up complaints is hard.
So many complaints make my insides feel bloated in a funny way.

Ichi felt as if her insides were swollen and distended with black gas from all the grievances. Yunami said the list wasn't mere discontent and grumbling but true words that would save them all, "words of God." Yunami and the other tenjins might have embraced the faith in someone called Lord Jesus that was now all the rage in the licensed quarter, Ichi thought.

"If the poor just go along unquestioningly with everything they're told," Yunami had said, "they'll never be saved." Maybe she was right.

"Aoi Ichi, copy the words on the blackboard."

Startled, Ichi jumped. "Yes'm."

After school, as Ichi walked by herself for a change, an old man called out to her from behind.

"Hey there! Kojika from the Shinonome, is it?"

"Yep, that's me. And?" She turned and faced him.

It was the old man from the hills who peddled sweets, his backpack full of sweet-potato candy and paste, malt-syrup candy, and more. Ichi knew him by sight. He glanced around before taking out what appeared to be a letter and handing it to her.

"Nazuna asked me to give this to you."

"What? Where is she?"

Nazuna's whereabouts had remained unknown ever since she had bolted on the way back from visiting Murasaki and her baby. Ichi had assumed she was somewhere remote, cut off from all communication.

"She wants you to send a reply. I'll come again tomorrow and wait for you here."

So the old peddler would be making his rounds again tomorrow. There was no writing on the front of the envelope. Scrawled on the back in small letters was "Sakihama Sue," Nazuna's real name.

To avert suspicion, Ichi brought out her change purse and bought a piece of hard candy, then walked back to the Shinonome sucking on it as she went. She went to the storage room, away from everyone, took out the letter, and read it behind a pile of futons.

Nazuna had written painstakingly, altering their names for fear the letter might get into the wrong hands.

Dear Shika,

Sorry for not writing. I'm living in the countryside, doing farmwork. Thanks to the oiran and her mister, I am living life to the fullest with all my energy.

All my friends are here, too. The oiran's baby got big.

I heard about the strike at the Shinonome. Never mind about that. Hurry and come.

From now on, the police have to allow prostitutes to give up their trade if they want. Her mister says so, and he's on the prefectural assembly, so it must be true. The world has changed.

Write soon. I can't wait to hear from you.

From Na-no-ji

The letter was short on details, but Ichi understood that Nazuna had safely escaped, that she was doing farmwork somewhere in the countryside, and that she was fine. She was amazed to learn these things.

There is a God!

This letter from her long-missing friend had come out of nowhere, as though brought by a bird from heaven.

Nazuna had not revealed where she was. The old candy peddler must know. Wherever it was, Murasaki was there, too, the wife or mistress of a man who was giving refuge to Nazuna and her friends.

Ichi remembered that among the clients at the Shinonome was the chairman of the prefectural assembly and several assemblymen, too. Now it was all beginning to make sense. One of those men must be the father of Murasaki's child. The friends Nazuna had mentioned must be other runaways like herself. Were they all living together now under one roof, supported by Murasaki's "mister"?

Though short on details, the letter made Ichi's heart beat faster. She felt a wind blowing in from outside. A wind that Nazuna had brought. What should she do now? How should she reply?

Nazuna was waiting for an answer.

Ichi tiptoed out of the storage room.

In the morning, the list of names on the refectory door had lengthened.

Matsunose
Hotaru

Usagi
Botan
Tsuruji
Harutake

More and more prostitutes were signing on to the strike. Those who would be working today had long since finished breakfast and headed off to the bathhouse. Those not working sat around leisurely chatting while snacking on confections and steamed sweet potatoes. For once, they had nothing to do. They were utterly relaxed and tranquil, full of anticipation as they wondered aloud whose names would be added next.

Hajima Mohei's continued silence was unsettling. Perhaps what Nazuna had written in her letter was true. Perhaps the police were now accepting prostitutes' formal statements of intent to quit the business, and that tied Mohei's hands.

The chatter in the room suddenly stopped. Ichi sensed a presence behind her as sweet perfume filled the air. She turned and saw Shinonome and Tamagiku standing there. Tamagiku removed the lid of a writing box, and Shinonome took out a brush and dipped it in ink. Everyone's eyes were glued to her hands.

Shinonome
Tamagiku

They both added their names. Shinonome's writing was as slender as grass and full of spirit; Tamagiku's was rounded and charming. A murmur went up among the prostitutes watching from a distance. Saito took in the entire scene from his doorway, gawking in helpless astonishment, and then rushed back into the office.

Just after noon, Ichi emerged from the Shinonome, followed by Shinonome and Tamagiku. Hailstones pelted them, borne on the wind. Ichi shook herself like a dog as she walked along.

They were on their way to the school to see Ichi's teacher. The four of them, Shinonome, Tetsuko, Ichi, and Tamagiku, had things they needed to talk over.

Ichi didn't feel the cold one bit.

I'll Die on the Waves

The familiar morning aroma of steamed rice wafted upstairs from the kitchen, bothering Ichi as she woke up and dressed. She hadn't had rice for breakfast for two weeks now since she joined the strike.

When she had finished dressing, she took out the note she'd brought back from school the day before and checked the items that the teacher had asked her to buy: "Straw sandals, gloves, gaiters, hats, and hand towels, 35 of each."

The supplies were for those scheduled to flee the Shinonome that night. Of the brothel's eighty prostitutes, nearly half had joined the strike and would walk out together. The rest were still uncommitted. The strike organizers, Yunami and Shibagaki, did not push them. They believed that in time, a second and a third wave of prostitutes would rise up and flee.

Mohei showed no sign of either stopping them from leaving or pushing them out the door. After the 1872

Livestock Emancipation Law, the road had been long and winding, but now, finally, the police had broken with the brothel owners association, leaving it to fend for itself. According to Tetsuko, the police had been ambushed by the unexpected alliance of the prefectural assembly, the women's movement, and the Salvation Army.

Soon Kogin and Umekichi joined Ichi, and the three of them went out together. After satisfying their hunger as usual at the udon shop, they went to the Higoya, just off Nakamise Avenue, and made the necessary purchases.

The exodus was set for late that night. Once safely past the great gate, the escapees would walk all night long. By dawn, the village where Nazuna and the former oiran Murasaki were waiting for them would come into view, said their guide, the old candy peddler who had reached out to Ichi. He told no one, Ichi included, the name of the village where they were going.

When the three returned to the Shinonome with their arms full of packages, they found a lively street performance in full swing. A trio of men dressed in black were dancing and playing music. One shook a large bell, one played a shiny flute, and the other beat a large drum strapped to his chest.

"It's the Salvation Army!" Umekichi was beside herself with excitement.

The music was bright and exhilarating, nothing like

the music of the shamisen and hand drum heard daily in the licensed quarter. The sounds were high-pitched and penetrating. The men sang in time to the music: *All who have lost your way, come here.*

Fascinated, they went closer for a better look. Up and down the street, faces clustered at second- and third-story windows. Then all of a sudden the musicians in black stopped singing and playing. A hush fell over the area. One of the men stepped toward the Shinonome and began loudly declaiming: "Women of the Shinonome, congratulations! Though you are the weaker sex, by going on strike, you are fighting like men. Bravo!"

Masseurs, hairdressers, medicine peddlers, entertainers, servants—everyone passing by clapped and jeered. Clearly, none of them were religiously inclined.

"The Salvation Army supports and encourages all prostitutes in the name of God. The charms you peddle are fleeting. Cease trusting in worthless men who seek only their own pleasure, place your trust in the true God in heaven, and quit this wanton business right away. In the name of God, choose the path of honest living. God is with you."

When the talk ended, the head-spinning music started up again, at once happy, plaintive, and somehow comical.

"Did you hear what he said? God is on our side." Kogin clasped her hands at her breast.

"What was that all about?" said Ichi. "When did we ever put our trust in men?" She kicked up some dirt. Who on earth would peddle their charms for the fun of it? Who would enter freely into this business? The God of these men had never seen how prostitutes lived.

"Dammit. Dammit!"

Music and singing drowned out her cries.

Fighting to save compatriots from ruin,
never yielding, marching ever onward goes
the Salvation Army.
Onward, onward, hallelujah!

"Dammit! Dammit!" Ichi was disgusted. Kogin and Umekichi each grabbed her by an arm and dragged her inside the Shinonome.

Up on the third floor, they found the other strikers waiting for them. Here, too, the Salvation Army music could be clearly heard. Some of the women were looking out the window at the street below, but none of them were infuriated like Ichi. Even though the performance was directed at them, they kept looking on in amusement. This made Ichi all the madder.

"My, what a temper!" Umekichi laughed.

"Never mind," said Kogin. "Let's pass out the straw sandals."

They untied the packages they had brought and began distributing the contents.

Then the tenjin Yunami came in, looking distracted. "We'll be walking all night tonight. Straw sandals won't be enough. Wrap your feet well. None of us have done much walking since we started working here." She took a pair of sandals and tried them on.

"It gets cold at night, so wear as many layers as you can. A quilted coat would be just the thing, if you have one. Wind the towel around your head and neck to stay warm, okay? Also, we've got to fortify our stomachs before we leave. Something hot would be good. One of you go to Gombei's and buy plenty of *amazake*. My treat."

The sweet, hot drink made of fermented rice would indeed fortify them. The big-sisterly tenjin was someone you could depend on. After issuing these detailed instructions, she left the room in a flurry. By then the Salvation Army music had stopped. Everyone dispersed to finish getting ready in their rooms.

Born and raised on an island in the warm southern sea, Ichi didn't own a quilted coat, but Shinonome had once sewn her a sleeveless jacket, along with a matching one for Tamagiku. She would wear that.

Before returning to her room, she went out into the small garden out back. Withered grasses lined the edge of the little pond. The crucian carp, tiny frogs, and diving beetles she had seen there recently were nowhere to be seen. They must be hibernating. "Stay well, everybody," she murmured, pushing aside grasses with her hands but finding no little creatures. A sheet of white ice, something she had never seen on her home island, covered the pond. She reached out and touched it. The ice was hard.

Had they suffocated to death? *Hang on! Ichi'll save you!*

She picked up a big stone and hurled it with both hands, smashing the ice and sending up huge jets of spray. Instantly, swirls of tiny water creatures came surging up. They were alive! The diving beetles' legs frantically churned the water. The frogs leaped, the crucian carp whirled.

"Everybody okay?" Ichi squatted down and leaned over the water. Then, slowly, her eyes focused on the surface of the pond. There in miniature she saw Umekichi, Kogin, and Yunami, as tiny as peas, spinning around and around in mad joy.

That night, Ichi sat at her desk and ground ink amid profound quiet, feeling as if all the people had vanished from the face of the earth. For the last few days, Tetsuko had had affairs to attend to, and classes had been canceled.

Tamagiku was absorbed in her nightly skin care

routine, rubbing her face and neck with soft red silk. Shinonome was in the adjoining room writing letters, perhaps apologizing to special clients for her sudden departure.

December 7 Sunny Aoi Ichi
Tonight is my last night here.
Futon, tatami, shoji, toilet,
thank you for everything.
Thank you also to the well, the refectory,
and the garden pond.
Stay well, ants in the garden
and creatures in the pond.
Good luck to you all.
See you tomorrow!

She set down her brush and pondered that last line, written in her island's dialect. It had the force of "goodbye," yet mentioning "tomorrow" felt strange. She would definitely not be seeing any of these things tomorrow, or ever again. Then what should she write? After a few moments, she crossed out the last line.

Lying on her back in bed, Ichi felt something warm near her face and slowly opened her eyes. The light of a tiny glass lamp shone by her pillow, and there stood Shinonome, looking down at her.

"It's time. Get ready to go."

Instantly awake, Ichi sat up in bed. Tamagiku was already dressed and her futon was put away; she was wrapping up her belongings in a big square cloth. Shinonome wore a heavy raincoat over her kimono and a fleecy woolen muffler around her neck.

Ichi had done her packing the night before: a change of clothes, a set of fresh underwear and tabi socks, plus one or two personal items. All that remained was her precious writing box and her small savings. Even so, the cloth bundle was bulging. She shouldered it and went out into the hallway. Shibagaki and Yunami came out of their room so thickly dressed in padded coats they looked like a pair of round Daruma dolls. They, too, carried big bundles on their backs.

"We don't look like oirans and tenjins anymore!" Shinonome smiled. "I used to imagine the day I would leave this place. Never did I dream it would be in the middle of the night with no one to see me off." She descended the stairs slowly as she spoke.

Downstairs, a cluster of women was waiting, each with a cloth bundle on her back. They looked like a pack of thieves in the night. Shinonome gave the signal with a look: *Let's go.* They moved toward the front door.

Saito, Mohei, and Tose all slept at home; only the male servants, the cooks, and Otoku were here overnight. Not being in positions of responsibility, they slept well. The male servants, who prided themselves on their physical strength, slept so soundly you could hardly shake them awake.

"Oiran, please wait!" Someone came running downstairs. It was a woman in her nightclothes, gasping for breath. As she came closer, they saw it was the tenjin Yumihachi. "What a waste for you to leave like this, when an eminent man is about to pay off your debt and set you free."

"I have earned more than my share here," said Shinonome. "I made this place rich. Mohei can have no cause to complain if I go. Now I want to live as I please. I'm sick of seeing clients."

"That's all very well, but what about the others? How are they supposed to live? If they go back home, their parents will only sell them again. A woman on her own in an unfamiliar place has no way to make an honest living." Yumihachi was in tears. "They'll end up selling themselves under the willows by the river. Life here may be painful, but at least they have a roof over their heads and food to eat. At New Year's they get a bit of extra money, and they can step out with the master's blessing. Make them change their minds. You've got to think of what's best for them!"

Ichi looked at Shinonome. Only participants in the strike knew that they did have somewhere to go, that Murasaki had prepared a place for them all to stay.

But sharing this information now with Yumihachi was impossible.

Shinonome stepped forward without hesitation. “We have thought this through, and our minds are made up. We are all going.”

Yumihachi’s face contorted. She cried out to the others, “Don’t go! Once you leave here, you’re finished. Don’t let the oiran lead you on!”

Shinonome took another step forward. The others did, too, forcing Yumihachi to retreat. Then from the darkened office came the sound of someone coming toward them, footsteps firm on the wooden floor. Hajima Mohei appeared in his nightclothes with a wrap around his shoulders. Apparently he had chosen to sleep here, sensing something was in the air. Trembling, the women distanced themselves from Shinonome.

Shinonome and Mohei stood facing one another. To Ichi, Shinonome looked as thin and frail as a candle wick. For the first time, she felt pity for her.

“Oiran, have I ever treated you badly?” Mohei’s voice seemed to echo as if emerging from a deep, dark cistern.

Shinonome shook her head.

“Have I ever cheated you or lied to you?”

She was silent.

“Have I even once cheated any of the women who work for me, the way others do?”

True, Ichi thought, Mohei was not a harsh master.

When one of them got sick he would send for a doctor, even if the patient herself bore the fee. He never dumped a dying prostitute in the compound of the neighborhood temple. He charged them for their kimonos, but he also made sure they dressed better than other prostitutes in the quarter. The futons he provided were warm. His wife, Tose, wasn't sly or dishonest, either.

"Nevertheless," said Shinonome, lifting her head and looking him straight in the eye, "you have bought and sold human beings."

Mohei didn't move.

Without another word, Shinonome turned toward the front door. Ichi and the rest followed her. She stepped down into the entryway and unbolted the door. A blast of wintry December wind swept inside. In the dark, the road outside was like a dark and bottomless river. She stepped outside, and one by one they followed her into the dark river.

"Goodbye!" each one said, turning back to look up at the Shinonome looming silently behind them. The deep black of the sleeping building blotted out a wide swath of the night sky.

"See you tomorrow," Ichi started to say but stopped herself. "Goodbye," she said, like everyone else. There would be no more tomorrows.

They streamed down Nakamise Avenue. Not even a dog stirred. At the great gate, they halted and braced themselves. Escape was impossible unless they succeeded in getting past this barrier. A guard was always on watch, and prostitutes entering or leaving the quarter were required to show a pass issued by their master. Those without a pass had no choice but to dive into the wide, fast-flowing Shirakawa River. But now it was winter. Before a swimmer could make it to the other side, she would be dead of hypothermia.

The guard, whose name was Tetsuzo, came out to talk to them. His right cheek bore the scar of a sword slash. Years before, he had stabbed to death a woman who spurned his attentions, but in prison his straightforward disposition had won favor, and on release he had secured this job. Knowing that he had murdered a colleague of theirs, the women of the quarter were afraid of him.

"Well, if it isn't the oiran of the Shinonome."

Ichi couldn't take her eyes off the stout oak stick in his hand.

"Where are you all tromping off to, decked out like this?"

Tetsuzo surveyed the group, taking in their unusual getups. The hubbub earlier that day from members of the Salvation Army had put him on alert. He prodded Shinonome deliberately to see how she would respond. Just behind Shinonome, the others trembled, as did the big bundles on their backs.

"We are running away." Shinonome spoke with poise.

"You don't say! And just where do you all plan to run off to?"

"Tonight we will take temporary shelter with the Salvation Army, and first thing tomorrow morning, we will go to the police."

Tetsuzo's face fell. Ever since the resolution taken up at the prefectural meeting the month before, local police had come under fire for impeding prostitutes from abandoning their profession if they wished to do so. Brothel owners no longer had the upper hand. Tetsuzo had heard all this from the association. The appeals of the Salvation Army and women's groups were rocking the prefectural assembly.

Tetsuzo stood frozen in dismay. How had such a thing come about? When had the licensed quarter lost its clout in society?

Lately, women from good families who knew nothing of the world had taken to crying in shrill voices, "Save the prostitutes!" and the Salvation Army had begun delivering sermons on street corners calling for prostitutes' emancipation. The world was turning upside down, it seemed to Tetsuzo. The life went out of him. He felt bleak and dejected.

"Tetsuzo," said Shinonome in a quiet tone, "we all must die one day and be held to account for how we lived. Tonight you have a chance to do something good."

She was addressing a man who had once taken a human life.

Tetsuzo stared at Shinonome. Then he removed the lock from the great gate. The heavy doors creaked open. The black line of women passed through and headed straight across the long bridge over the river, its surface glistening white in the moonlight. The sound of the women's footsteps was lost in the roar of rushing water.

On the other side of the bridge, two figures were waiting for them. Tetsuko was there, as promised, and at her side was the old candy peddler.

"All has gone according to plan," said Tetsuko. "Well done, everyone. From here on, Kihachi will lead the way to the village where we are going. We have to walk all night, so try to keep up as best you can. By the time the sun comes up in the morning, we will be there, and a hot meal will be waiting for us."

Murmurs of relief spread through the group.

Kihachi took the lead. Behind him Tetsuko and Shinonome walked side by side, followed by the threesome of Ichi, Tamagiku, and Umekichi.

Ichi was concerned about how Shinonome's legs would hold up, since the oiran was unused to walking. An all-night hike was asking a lot of her. But if she traveled by rickshaw, the driver would be able to reveal where they had gone.

All at once Kihachi's figure disappeared from view.

The road entered a bamboo forest, and soon Ichi and the rest were also engulfed in darkness, as if they'd stumbled into a black pit. Only the dim light of a lantern here and there penetrated the gloom. Tamagiku's small hand gripped Ichi's tighter.

The bamboo forest felt endless, as if they were creeping on and on through an underground cavern. To ward off the oppression of the heavy darkness, they spoke in undertones.

"After I get there," said Umekichi, "I'm going to help on the farm. I'm really, really looking forward to it." Her voice was warm. "I can plant rice or tend crops or do anything they want. I may be bad in bed, but I can grow vegetables like you wouldn't believe!"

Giggles from her companions sounded in the darkness.

"Where are you from, Umekichi?" Ichi had never asked her this before. Seeing her colleagues' faces and necks coated with thick white face powder, it had never occurred to her that any of them had a hometown.

"My folks are farmers in Chikushi. Farmers can survive without money, as long as they have seeds to plant. They can eat whatever they grow."

"Really?" Ichi was doubtful. The only seeds that came to her mind were seeds of melons and gourds. The island where she'd grown up was small, with little arable land. "What can you grow from seeds?"

"What? You don't know? Daikons, pumpkins, and carrots, for starters. Rice and barley, too. Everything grows from seeds. Even people."

Ichi was jealous. Seeds grew in fields—all but people seeds, of course. There were no fields in the sea. But if such things as parrotfish seeds, grunt seeds, large-scale blackfish seeds, and greater amberjack seeds existed, then the sea was the field where they were sowed. A field on top of the waves. The southern sea was a deep and powerful blue, different from the sea around here. Ichi pictured it in her mind. With waters so rich and abundant, how come islanders, her parents included, were all so poor?

"You're from a southern island, Ichi, aren't you?" said Umekichi. "What kinds of things live in the sea?"

"Parrotfish, flying fish, striped jack, grunt, wrasse, prawns, and bonito."

"What are those?" Umekichi looked puzzled.

Ichi was appalled at this ignorance. "Different kinds of fish, of course!"

Umekichi still seemed bewildered. She gave a dry laugh. "If a farmer and a fisherman traded places, neither one would know up from down, would they?"

"You can say that again." Ichi nodded in the darkness. "I wish there really were seeds for flying fish and striped jack."

"Okay." Umekichi thought Ichi was being silly.

"You see," Ichi said dreamily, "if there were seeds for grunt and wrasse, I could've planted them in the sea, and then my pa wouldn't have had to sell me."

"But in life, sometimes there are problems that grunt and wrasse can't solve," Umekichi, the older of the two, said soberly.

"Problems that planting rice doesn't help, either?"

"That's right."

During lulls in the conversation, their surroundings became again a pitch-black cavern lit only by a lantern here and there.

"When we get where we're going, you could work in the fields, too, Ichi."

Ichi hesitated to reply to this invitation. She wasn't sure she would be any good at farming. But if she were to stay at Murasaki's place, she would have to learn. As the tenjin Yumihachi had said when trying so desperately to stop them from leaving, those with no skills would be forced to go back to being prostitutes. And next time, they would end up in a truly unspeakable hell.

Me, plant daikons? Maybe that was her destiny after all. Where else could she go except Murasaki's place?

They fell silent again, plodding on through the thick darkness. Then from behind, Kogin said, "I'm not going to be a farmer. I'm going to work for God."

"For God?" Umekichi turned and looked back at her. "You can't make a living that way."

"I heard that if you go to the Salvation Army, they'll give you a place to stay and work to do."

This set them all chattering, until Umekichi spoke up: "What kind of work can a former prostitute do to earn her keep? Wouldn't you be better off working in the fields or tending silkworms?"

"I won't know exactly till I go to the Salvation Army and ask." Kogin's tone was calm and reasonable. "After we get settled in our new place, I mean to go to town and find out."

This young woman's heart now belonged firmly to the god named Jesus.

"I can survive without parents, as long as I have God."

Kogin continued to talk about God as they walked along. Perhaps he was a light in the darkness for her. The others listened quietly.

"My father sold me, but I don't need him. I have the Lord Jesus. I have no mother anymore, but I have Mother Mary."

"Where are they?" asked Ichi.

"Inside me." Kogin tapped her chest.

Ichi countered by tapping her own chest with pride. "I have a god inside me, too. The god of the sea."

Tamagiku, who had kept silent until now, looked up in surprise. "You have a god, too, Ichi?"

"He's not only mine. He belongs to everyone on my island."

"What's he like?"

"He's the god of Watatsumi Palace."

"Watatsumi?"

"Another name for Ryugu-jo, the dragon palace. He's Urashima, the god of everyone who works in the sea. There's a goddess called Otohime, too."

Urashima and Otohime were like Jesus and Mary.

"The Lord Jesus has angels for vassals," said Kogin. "They look just like humans, but they have big white wings on their backs."

Ichi was not to be outdone. "The vassals in Watatsumi Palace are sea turtles. The god of sea turtles has a long tail that's divided in seven."

In Ichi's house, there'd been an image of that god up on the wall. The shell on his back, said to be as big as a tatami mat, was covered with shining green moss. His seven tails were long, thick, and hairy. She had heard some fishermen who nearly drowned in a storm say that when they sank to the bottom of the sea, the turtle appeared and saved them by letting them grab hold of one of his tails.

"I saw him with my own eyes once, too," said Ichi. "The sea was filled with sparkling light and jewels like pearls. He swam ever so slowly and turned the water around him as dark as evening."

She said this in a loud voice, and the others scoffed.

Ichi pouted. She'd heard that Jesus took the form of a man and floated up into the sky. Well, why shouldn't the god of the sea appear in the sea? Which was more ridiculous? She shook her head, perplexed.

But oh, this darkness!

Ichi looked up and caught a glimpse of sky in the narrow space between the trees. The forest went on and on with no apparent end, from darkness to darkness. To avoid potential pursuers, they had taken a remote path through the mountains.

After several hours they came to a small forest shrine. Old Kihachi opened the shrine door and let everyone inside, and then he handed out rice balls. Tetsuko removed Shinonome's and Tamagiku's sandals and rubbed ointment on the soles of their feet.

Shinonome and Tamagiku discussed the strike while eating. Listening without really meaning to, Ichi gathered that someone named Fukuzawa Yukichi disapproved of strikes.

"Apparently," said Tetsuko, frowning, "he says that we cannot build a strong country by paying heed to every claim of the uneducated poor."

"But isn't listening to the opinions of only the rich and powerful dangerous for both the country and the people?"

As Tetsuko and Shinonome continued speaking in low voices, Ichi put her arms around Tamagiku and dozed.

When the way grew lighter in the gray predawn, they saw an expanse of winter fields and shining rivers dotted with dark patches of woods and thatched roofs below the winding mountain path. Shedding their fatigue, they erupted in hoarse cheers and cries of joy.

The group made its way down the mountainside and past the grove of the village shrine, coming finally to an imposing gated residence. Hearing voices outside, several farmers came out to greet them, followed by Murasaki. She, too, was dressed in farmer's work clothes and a sleeveless jacket of padded cotton. She and Shinonome ran toward each other and grasped each other by the hands. Everyone trooped inside and sat down to a hot breakfast prepared by village women.

Murasaki's husband had gone to Kumamoto and wouldn't be back until that evening, she said. "You must all be exhausted after walking all night long. Please lie down and rest or take a nap, as you please."

Servants brought in futons and laid them out. There were a lot of women working in the residence. Work seemed plentiful.

Then Tetsuko brought out a list of names. She read each participant's name aloud, along with her place of birth, and had them divide up by geographical location. They needed to make decisions about their futures. Rather than have the thirty-five of them spread out randomly, it made more sense to have people from the same vicinity stick together.

The women of Kyushu formed four groups: Chikushi,

Hyuga, Higo, and Satsuma. Several others were from the Kyoto-Osaka area. Shinonome, Tamagiku, and Tetsuko joined that group.

From Satsuma there were three islanders: Ichi from Iojima; Yubune, a fisherman's daughter from neighboring Takeshima, who had arrived earlier that year; and Sammaru, a farmer's daughter from Kirishima. They lay down and started talking. Sammaru said that if she went home, there wouldn't be enough to eat, so she wanted to stay and work in Murasaki's residence.

If Sammaru went home, she would be sold again, thought Ichi. She was going on fourteen and still barely knew how to apply face powder. If Ichi went home and told her parents she had run away, her father would be certain to hit the roof. Going home before you had fulfilled the terms of your contract was a disgrace.

As Ichi and Yubune sat there at loose ends, their futures unsettled, an older girl named Tomoe came over and asked if they were the Satsuma amas. She was from the island of Genkai in Chikushi, she said, and invited them to go there with her.

"My pa's dead, and my ma and little sister work as amas. I just got word from Ma. Amas like us have always gone to Jeju Island to work, and she says the two of them are going next year. I reckon I'll go, too." Amas all across western Japan were moving to the island just south of Korea, Tomoe said, where the waters were rich in mackerel and horse mackerel. “Every island wants divers like us. What do you say? Let’s go! An all-women fishing ground would be great!”

Before Tomoe had finished speaking, Yubune declared herself in. Ichi stared into space, unable to decide. Her father’s thin, sunburned face rose in her mind. What if she went home laden with presents? Maybe then her family would take her back.

“I’m in, too.” Suddenly her mind was made up.

“Wonderful!” said Tomoe. “Let’s drink on it! The three of us will stick together!”

Tomoe brought out a narrow bamboo container from her sleeve, filled the lid with sake, and handed it first to Ichi. *What foresight*, Ichi thought with admiration. The small lid passed from Ichi to Yubune and back to Tomoe, who soon returned to her original group.

After she was gone, Yubune lay down alongside Ichi. They both felt relieved and confident they’d made the right decision, as if they’d boarded a boat that would transport them safely ashore. All around the room, others were deep in conversation. The boats of some had apparently set sail, while others remained temporarily stranded. The room gradually quieted down. Outside, the sun was up, but inside, everyone’s eyelids were heavy.

Ichi drifted off to sleep. In water shot through with sunlight and pearl-like bubbles, she saw the seven-tailed sea turtle from Watatsumi Palace come gliding toward her. She cast off all her clothes and became as smoothly naked as a fish. It felt good.

"Thank you, everyone." In her dream, Ichi offered thanks to no one in particular.

Translator's Note

A Woman of Pleasure was originally published in 2013 and received the 65th Yomiuri Prize for Fiction. It is a work of fiction based on true events, written by one of Japan's most celebrated novelists. In language charged with the beauty and force of poetry, Murata Kiyoko takes us into the life and mind of fifteen-year-old Aoi Ichi, sold by her father into prostitution from the tiny island of Iojima (known in the West as Iwo Jima) at the turn of the twentieth century. The Shinonome was an exclusive brothel in the Nihongi pleasure district of Kumamoto on the southern island of Kyushu. That storied world is re-created in remarkable detail, with unforgettable portraits of a panoply of women—everyone from the beautiful Kannon-like oiran at the top down to hapless girls at the bottom plagued with mounting debts, along with the occupational hazards of "knobby backside" and worse. The novel's memorable opening pages give a sobering indication of the indignities and trials that lie ahead for Ichi and the other newcomers.

Amid these difficulties, Ichi finds comfort and courage in her memories of life on her idyllic island, where she swam in blue waters alongside giant sea turtles and dolphins; in her friendships with the other girls, not to mention with ants in the garden; and above all in mandatory classes at the nearby Female Industrial School, where her beloved teacher, Akae Tetsuko, aims to inculcate not just literacy but also habits of clear thinking and self-expression. In 1901, the Kumamoto brothel owners association did in fact establish such a school for the benefit of women working in the pleasure quarter, as required by law. Ichi, arriving in 1903, attends classes daily and keeps a journal where, with simplicity and insight, and writing in her native dialect, she sets down her observations and reactions to her new life. The entries are the highlights of each chapter, functioning rather like the envoys or summary tanka that follow long poems in the *Man'yoshu*. Her appealing teacher is an independent thinker who admires the progressive views of the educator Fukuzawa Yukichi—famous for his declaration "Heaven does not create one person above another"—but is infuriated when she realizes that his definition of "person" applies only to the upper classes.

He writes off women working in the licensed quarter as "not human to begin with." Under Tetsuko's guidance, Ichi blossoms.

Ultimately, Ichi joins a labor strike triggered by the prostitutes' irritation at the high price they are forced to pay for tobacco. Soon the strikers come up with a comprehensive list of demands. In the last chapter, some forty women band together and go on a daring night trek led by the oiran and the schoolteacher in search of new lives. As the novel shows, this historic event, memorialized in a popular ditty called "The Shinonome Strike," was inspired in part by a labor strike at a nearby Nagasaki shipyard. What happened to the original strikers we do not know, but those in the book seem to have an excellent chance of remaking their lives for the better. The strike is the perfect culmination of Ichi's journey of self-discovery.

Murata expertly presents Ichi's story in its full historical and social context. Readers may be interested to see the role played by the Salvation Army in encouraging prostitutes to aim higher in life. We associate the Salvation Army of today with thrift shops and street-corner donations of red kettles at Christmastime, but in late Meiji Japan, under the leadership of Yamamuro Gumpei, the first Japanese officer of the Salvation Army, the organization fought for the abolition of public prostitution and pushed for social reform. Christian doctrine also serves as a foil for Ichi's beliefs rooted in Japanese folklore, especially the myth of the Ryugujo, the underwater palace of the dragon god of the sea.

Translating Ichi's writings was a particular challenge, since her dialect, containing "traces of the Satsuma-Osumi dialect, but . . . a little different," verges on the incomprehensible. Ichi is continually chided for talking "bird talk," or squawking like a chicken. Murata, herself a native of Fukuoka, uses dialect to give authenticity and richness to the story; annotative glosses known as ruby convey the meaning in standard Japanese. Generally, I think there is little to be gained by trying to duplicate Japanese dialect in English, and even if that were remotely possible here, it would make the book extremely hard to read. For Ichi's writing, I used standard spelling and contented myself with providing hints, such as the omission of punctuation marks, to remind the reader that she is still learning. Making her compositions barely readable would distract from the wonderful content, and anyway no English dialect that I am aware of could possibly convey how alien Ichi sounds. As always, the reader's imagination must come into play—just as the reader must imagine how Ichi's writing resembles "wriggly" worms on the page, while the oiran's is like "an arrangement of beautiful vines."

It has been my great honor to translate this superb

novel dealing with the feelings and struggles of women from 120 years ago in Japan, written by a master of the art of fiction. Despite the progress that has been made in the interim, women's struggles continue today. May this book strike a chord with readers everywhere.

JULIET WINTERS CARPENTER
September 2023

KIYOKO MURATA was born in Fukuoka, Japan, in 1945. She has been awarded more than ten major literary awards in Japan, including the Akutagawa Prize in 1987. *A Woman of Pleasure* is Murata's first book to be published in English.

© Toyota Horiguchi

JULIET WINTERS CARPENTER is professor emerita at Doshisha Women's College of Liberal Arts in Kyoto and has received numerous awards for her translation work, including the 2021–2022 Lindsey and Masao Miyoshi Translation Prize for lifetime achievement as a translator of modern Japanese literature. She lives on Whidbey Island in Washington State.